A man who's tired of London is
tired of institutional aggression
chicken carcasses littering the streets
black rubber in public spaces

CHUBZ
The Demonization of My Working Arse
by Spitzenprodukte

MONTEZ PRESS

For Rifal and ffuckpig,
and puremania, and others,
whose usernames I forget
but whose data has stained

CHAPTER 1

The most satisfying way to kill someone with a baseball bat isn't two-handed, like in films. Rather, it's to swing the bat high with one hand, then let gravity help you pull it down in an arc, playing against the tension of the wrist, smashing into your victim with an easy velocity. Putting your shoulder into it, like fist-pumping the floor. It's just more satisfying. Peculiarly satisfying. It was this sort of satisfaction that Mike was alluding to when he sent me text messages, especially the early morning ones.

Mike called me Andrew which is fair enough but the only people who don't call me Chubz is work so I guess that should have set the tone. Please don't get me wrong we had no arrangement. I liked him because he was hot. Not too pushy. The night we met we'd been chatting online for maybe a week because he took his time (was romantic). And I'd given him my number.

Our whatsapp log was busy and tense. The tone came in waves, conversational and flirty then you can almost pinpoint the minute he gets his dick out because bang bang bang the messages come fast, quick, one hand sniper

> I want to pound you,
>   pound yr hole

In this mood, he switched easily between genders in his texts.

> Give me yr hole,
>   you slut. Be a good
>   girl and take
>   my pounding

I'd woken late, with my duvet around my feet and already hard; I could hear people milling round the estate outside my window, kids on bikes at the start of their holidays I guess. The cages of the basketball court rattled. It sat in the middle of the square, trapped on three sides by the high rises, with light flooding in from the open end, where you could see across most of Bermondsey, almost to the river. My bedroom opened out on to the balcony, where I hung my pants to dry in weather like this. I could almost feel the old building baking in this heat. Doors that usually banged had started to warp. When you opened the chute, the stench of rotting rubbish was foul. I think a fox had died in there.

My curtain wasn't much use against the day; heat blazed in around the edges and I started to wank. I pulled my hand around my ballsack and thought about getting laid, rolling over to check my phone, red dot for 'Mike's hard', message back.

hey it's Andy. You
still wanna meet?

Andy was for use with teachers, Mum, feds and new fucks. The rest of the day I was Chubz. I was a fat kid till I was 19. I'd lost it, pushed it down, weaponised it in the form of a butt.

yeah, I thought
maybe you
were being flakey

nah just been busy
innit

He gave me his location, the street name, flats down in Shoreditch. The heat came up for the streets harder than it came down from the sun, and I jumped a bus that was full of fleshy people, that buzzed with tin beats from little in-ears and everyone wore short sleeves and short dresses and my dick filled up with the fact that the heat made the city into sex. Rolling off the bus the street was nice, cooler from the tall flats along the thin old street, rebuilt like this whole part of the city with big windows, small balconies, expensive plants frying in the sunlight, frosted glass and shared entrances, garage doors with bullshit posh graffiti, thick double yellow lines barely 3 yards apart and scooters resting up by lampposts. I looked hot, had three days off, my skin tingled with new burn and I wanted to get my legs open. I threw my empty can down the street.

I buzzed and waited.

— hello?

— Hey, it's Andy

— Hey, it's Flat 44

I like your flat, I said. It was very bouji, cheap luxury, you know. Nothing delicious and seedy. I needed a keycode. He was a tall man, wearing a shirt. White, professional, his hair brushed back across his head and he kept fiddling with his shirt-cuffs. He led me in to his sitting room, and I sat, and he disappeared, nervously looking for jobs to do, as if I'd disturbed him; a nervous man used to being confident, in charge, has an air of recklessness about him.

I don't think calling him an aggressive top would really suffice; sex in meatspace doesn't perfectly reflect online profiles. He might pull my grey trackies down so they just showed me arse, and that'd be softly, with a nuzzle to my neck, but the tempo never lasted like that for long. He liked to bang, pound, stretch my hole, fill me. That's how it went, he owned my hole.

It wasn't till a week later, as I lay on the wooden floor of his living room whilst he found his clothes and went to the kitchen, that I realised I couldn't remember when it last rained. We hadn't had rain for at least 6 weeks, swear down. It was coming to the end of summer but even then, in London, for the air to get so dusty, to not have the street tamped down at least on occasional summer nights by a warm rain, seemed unusual. The heat brought with it smells, and that's what people had started talking about, the smell of dumpsters behind costcutters that filled the high street. I didn't mind the smells; they felt thick and natural for a city summer. But people were bristling on the street; women with bags off their arms, sunglasses slipping from greasy hair, snapping at Big Issue guys, cars skidding out of turns late at night; this big guy shouting from a top window as girls go past; it all mixes with the rotting meat and petrol, sticky iron tastes on your tongue and flowers decaying in the bins by the market.

Me and Mike fucked 3 or 4 more times, before I stopped texting him and he stopped texting me. He'd got to know what he wanted of me by then, and that's cool. Things have a shelf-life, and anyway, the streets were full of lads with their tops off, and some of them wanted me, at least. One time, 10 times, I'm cool.

The rest of the summer, though, overtook a good hookup like Mike. It was summer too hot for something that casual. A restlessness for something more meaningful meant I could have flitted between 100 men not knowing what I was trying to find with each, but something, something more meaningful. I guess I got it, but I gave it to everyone, sucked everyone in to my own personal change. The city changed because of a guy I met on grindr. Everything that flooded the gutters came from my hand that summer.

London's like a load of maps laid over one another; in my mind, a series of different lives like neighbourhoods, and neighbourhoods like lives, where angers and tears and joy sit upstairs and downstairs, on top of each other, where overheard radios and funerals knit into personal sentiments, where hand-holding and fights in bars meet. On top, I see bus routes and short cuts; below, a map of half-remembered days designated "good times" spread between parks and strangers bedrooms.

But for the past few months - maybe a year - a single layer that shifted, half-visible before, has become dominant, blotting out all other points I used in my head to navigate. I don't know how to phrase it; something like struggling for work and something like that exhaustion and something like - hey, let's not mince words here - the assault on proletarian London.

I walked back through the estates, the last time I saw Mike. Sweat ran from my lower back, mixing with the lube and spit that slid around my arse cheeks. In my head I planned out a few things for the next couple of days; work, looking for work, big shop from tescos, put a wash on, make some calls. That was my plan for the summer. Not going away this summer, not going anywhere I don't think. Round the corner from home, I hopped up the two tile steps into Lidl.

A man sweating through a pleather jacket stood in the aisle of Lidl. He span the bat in his hand, felt the weight of it pull against his wrist. It was still shrink-wrapped in a hard plastic packaging; at the tip of the bat, a cheap chinese-produced baseball was packaged too, like an apple sealed in plastic. I thought about how hard it would be for him to open when he got it home, how frustrating those durable plastic packs are. He grimaced, the edge of his mouth turning down in a smirk, and nodded his head. This would do. He also picked up a pack of AA batteries as he made his way to the till.

After I'd paid I left the shop and the sun prickled my face. On the steps under the canopy, the tallest of the security guards had stopped a young Asian woman. I paused to roll my t-shirt sleeves up and saw him arguing with her, snapping at her. He had stopped her for shoplifting; she hadn't taken anything, but he had thought she had. In good faith. I could just see her expression under her fur-lined polyester hood.

Her face was thick with a sickly foundation but her eyes had the panic of someone at the hard end of a mistake. I thought about Mike's flat, how nice it was. I wouldn't mind some of that, but have I gotta fuck someone like him to keep it? I left the path through the park and hopped the fence by my block. I'm literally never getting a flat like that, right? He had spent the last hour we'd had talking about work, sat up bare-chested in bed, talking about the future. I wasn't there, but I don't think I'm factored into anyone's future plans. In the future people like me don't exist; we're fun for the present, that's it.

I've never felt my mental state working up close with events in newspapers. That stuff has never been about me before. Tourists came and went, but I lived behind a cloud where possibility was totally limited, where potential, potential for control of change, was a fiction. But before all that, before I met this guy later that week, as I walked back from Mike's through the estate at the start of the heat, I reveled in being angry and useless. I didn't *want* a job this summer, I wanted to fuck, and I wanted stuff to kick off. I felt angry too, right. I enjoy impotent anger because it's the closest I come to refusing, to being different. Not making plans. I was tired of people on grindr or scruff telling me they were tired of people looking for casual sex, they wanted a boyfriend, they wanted a puppy, they wanted a house, they wanted kids. Yeah well you're not the only one who's tired, buddy, I wanted to reply. I'm not looking for casual sex either. I'm looking for something more meaningful too. Something like a conspiracy to commit public disorder.

CHAPTER 2

My dream is to be ruined as a man, plundered, taken from.

Hey, can I come
over? Free?

I'm into serving, I'm into being on me hands and knees on your floor as you fuck my mouth.

Fun? Accom? Hey?

Hey. Hot. How was
work? Hello.
Hey. Hi. Hi. Free?

Photo received.
Hi, nice. Any more
pics? Mmm, into piss
and pits too. Love it
all mate, feet piss rub.
Lucky u. Hung?

Good thanks. A bit
horny. Photo sent.
Nice to meet u.

I like arriving to find this particular body. Muscles just starting to push through a creamy white skin. Beard. A stomach, defined at the edges only. Restart your engines. Click here now. Click again. Refresh. Hey, refresh *yourself*. Click.

The chest is tight, skintight, taut, and the hairs short. Boxy, shorter guy, you look him from top to bottom - bristle black hair and beard and cheeky glint fella.

And under the skin these smoothed turns and bumps betray a bodily hulk and twitching power is in this flesh. Refresh, run your hand into your pants, pull at your bellend, scroll faster hey whatsup hey so this is where I live I want you to come round and push your cock down my throat fuck it use it fill me with your dick and cum in my face yeah yeah.

Your flesh is fast and tender and I need to taste you. You peel off your jeans and you're strapped with elastic. White crosses you, one side to another. It's stretched across this plane of flesh below your stomach, splits, diverges, runs across the small of your back, that hallowed place, and pulls down, this elastic, dive-bombing aerial across a hairy buttock, pulling back under that buttock, lost up in your ass crack, cupped into your inner thighs, leading my eye, click more, see more, hey, meet?

Green light, go,
suck my dick.

Report crash. Go to
homepage, rate me.
Round the front your
jock pulls up your
balls.

Black mesh, red piping, cotton polyester mix nestled in your nutty pubes, white and nutty thighs.

I lay back in bed reading your messages, flicking through the photos received, checking your location. We were geolocated as I took a bus through Stokey, but I think I'll get back on it to see you again, to drop to my knees, waddle towards you, flash you my whites, give it to me use my holes. Give me it! You step back I inch forward. GIVE ME IT you push my head back. I force you to force yourself on me. I make me your slave, I pray on my knees for a violence focused on me for a change, it's my mouth my hole you use you want to use you want to abuse it, it's me you've chosen to feel worthless, share, share with friends, like. Alright, I'll come round.

CHAPTER 3

I step on the bus from a pavement covered in ash and scrapings of dried dogshit. It pulls off, shaking me along the top deck; I wedge myself against the window at the back. The city draws itself past my seat: a couple walk down the street, her ponytail brushing between bra straps, his bare back framed by a cap and his boxer shorts. An older woman leans out the second floor window drawing on a fag. I'd done two hours overtime; my boss was acting the cunt all afternoon

— you do realise this is the sort of thing that's linked to your bonus Andrew

— I know and

— And I'll be writing your 6 month appraisal soon. Look I know it's a pain Andy, really, but it'd be really helpful if you could

Alright alright; two hours later, no pay guaranteed, I'm sick of this job already and I push my face against the window and feel the warm vibrations of the glass and the girls in front talking who each other are fucking. We stop at lights; days like this make me dizzy, my eyes too hot, tired and in need of instant response.

My smartphone needs to be squeezed from my pockets, and I swipe through my social networks. I load Grindr, ping through my messages; no, no, would suck but no, I load the feed, a mosaic of torsos; one wears a t-shirt and I can see a dark fleck I take for nipple through the white cotton. Lips are visible, just and a blue box appears in the corner. A message from the boy; this is how I met him, early in that summer heat, face worn out from work, beads of sweat meeting in my lower back. His name was Owen, and he sent me a facepic; cute, boyish, blonde hair surfing over delicious blue eyes.

My bus heaved through the traffic and my attention to the world around me began to sink away. I was locked in quick chat; four words pinged back, a sentence returned, I showed him by body and by the time the bus passed Sainsbury's I'd seen Owen's nipples, pink and light, blushing against the creamy tight skin of his torso. My mind was lost and around the inside of my mouth I could feel my muscles turning. Pools of saliva gathered under my tongue as I felt my bellend run up my inside thigh. The descriptions of what would happen to me were

I ever to fall into his hands pushed the blood back up to my face; I readjusted my cap and ran my hand down the front of my t-shirt, brushing past my nipples as I thought of his bone white torso on top of me, pushing against my rooftop tan. I bit my lips at the thought of running my hand through that dirty blonde hair, his lips pushed up between my legs, I closed my eyes for a second, let out of a deep exhale and rang the bell. Oh oh Owen, I need this; I send over my number.

I got home from my job at Costa in London Bridge that Sunday. Laying back on my sofa, feeling my back stick against the pleather cushions, and he texts;

Hello Andy, it's Owen.
Are we going to
make an evening of it?
His address followed, 10 minutes walk away
I'm free from 8
I checked my watch. 7:30.
sounds fun mate.
Give me an hour xox
The guy seemed well turned out.
It had been sunny now non-stop for weeks,

and on Saturdays we hung out in park usually, if I didn't have a shift, some girls from the estate who I'd known since school, some fags and some uni kids from nearby. The heat was starting to get to me, man. I wanted a load, so I'd called him on the walk back, as I jumped over the low hooped railings.

By the time I got to his my work was a bit more in focus; a flick through my post, a quick shower, the end of zoot from last night, and I was out on the street, clean sneakers, walking past the boys on the corner, on the bus, thinking about the photo Owen had sent me of his crisp chest, smooth and young, looking younger than his stats suggested. I walked up the stairs to his door, and pushed my thumb hard against the little plastic bell; I heard it gurgle at the back of the house then break into a full throated ring. There was a padding of feet in white sport socks scooting to the door.
— Hey, come on in

The house was nice, three storeys, rooms around a thin staircase stripped of carpet. He shared his house with others, from what I could guess. As soon as I arrived he'd taken me to his

room; I watched his arse push itself around his blue jeans as he climbed two steps at a time.
– Can I get you anything?

This strange chatter when you hook up bugs me man. Is it not enough to want a body? I got the basics: he was 30, 8 years older than me. He worked as a subeditor for a magazine. He worked for a think-tank focused on progressive taxation. He worked for an NGO. Nah, he was a journalist I think. I picked an office as my place of work and he didn't seem to care much beyond that right?

It was something like that, I can't remember: my mind flicked over his skin as he pulled off his shirt, wild pink nipples on the white. I felt his hands push my flesh into the cotton as he hurried himself, and that fear that men like him get with men like me. His thumbs push open his button fly and then open a hole in the fabric of his boxers, and under this a rush of sweet smell and pubes and his thumb hooks out an unexpected cock. It was substantial, I'd say, substantial enough that he knew this fat flesh had meaning. It was invested in being a cock, it knew its mind and as cocks go it was

what I wanted inside me right then and there.
He ran his hand through my hair, and I slide
it to the back of throat first time.

CHAPTER 4

Nigel Farage swigs deeply from his pint of Bombardier, stifling a content smile as the blokes throw their heads back in guffaws at his joke.

— Good man, Nigel!

chortles Tim, thrusting his hands deep into his pockets. Brian, Nigel's minder, taps him on the shoulder, a pre-agreed sign that the meet-and-greet must come to an end; catching his eye, Nige nods.

— Well, chaps, was great to hear you views. I couldn't agree more about capital investment. I trust UKIP has your vote in Gannet?

— Nigel, I'd be proud to

Brian offers; shaking hands, Nige grips Brian further down the arm. A frisson of masculine assurance passes through their body, as Brian catches a beery burp in the back of his mouth. The pub is swollen with hearty English cheer; the locals are proud to have the eyes of the world on them, as the shock-troops of the metropolitan elite push microphones and lenses towards them, desperate to catch their opinions. The bar is gleaming; each local ale boasts a bright handle with a different World War themed logo. Behind the bar, nestled between the scampi fries and peanut-girl, a Keep Calm and Carry On poster makes some glib joke about how shit it is to work here, how the boss is a fucking arsehole.

– This Is Hell

thinks Sally, cub reporter for *The Gatekeeper*, Britain's premium, unpaywalled liberal-left newspaper, and woman who feels a deep erotic repulsion at the sight of men in suits. Torn between the desire to catch the scoop her editor, Ian Busbridge, looks for - the one where Farage does something totally unheard of in the offices of *The Gatekeeper*

– and this physical compulsion to make true the emoji knife snapchats of the seedy, obscene underbelly of journalism, Sally follows Farage through the porch of The Knobs Head into the salty streets of Gannet North.

– Nigel, do you have anything to say about recent comments from your candidate in Brunwich about the unsuitability of women to exist?

– Ah Sally

his eye twinkled with futurelust

— From *The Gatekeeper*. How's Alexander doing?

The in-joke was lost on Sally, and her follow up question lost in the hoots of

— Nigel! Nigel!

From the mob of photographers hubble-clustered for a portrait of the rising star as he stepped from the pavement, his halo temporarily obscured by a cluster of Labour supporters holding red placards accusing him of representing the worst of Britain. Sally could taste the salt from the sea air pushing up her nose, cut through with a vinegary pong drifting up through the pub's kitchen window, behind the grill beneath her feet. A photographer pushed her; her heel slipped between the bars and she stumbled back against the wall, watching her scoop wave as he slipped down into his Merc. Shit, she thought. No real story. Nothing today. The car pulled away, Nige's shit-eating grin pushed against the window, reflected back through her subconscious for the rest of the night. He leaves behind a cloud of media, drifting apart like pulled pork, diluted by the crowds of drinkers leaving the pub.

— That *Gatekeeper* hack is a chippy old girl!

Nige roars to Melissa, his personal assistant, as his car cruises past housing estates pebble-dashed against the North Sea. Melissa ignores him; she sorts through her papers, thrusting the evening's itinerary into his hand. A dinner for donors at the country house hotel booked out for the week's campaigning. Nige loosens his tie, unbuttons his shirt jacket, and breathes out deeply.

— I have a good feeling about tonight, Melissa. I've been told Peter Buchanan (well known car dealer) is contemplating a rather significant donation to The Spitfire Fund. Wait till those Bolsheviks at the *Gatekeeper* get a sniff of that!

Melissa looks up from her iPhone. She's sure her fiancé didn't go back to their flat last night. Where has he been staying?

— Nigel, it's important you thank the Mayor's wife tonight. She's got a lot of influence in the town, and she was instrumental to organising this dinner. You'll get a lot of kudos if you keep her fans sweet. And whatever you do, no gay jokes please. Nothing approaching them. Their daughter came out as a lesbian last year and it's still a sore point with the local press.

29

Apparently the mayor didn't take it too well – Gosh! It's a den of inequity old Gannet North, isn't it?

His car crackled across the gravel as it pulled up to the hotel. There was a greeting party waiting for him; the Mayor's wife, visibly excited at his arrival, a bozo UKIP apparatchik in a new suit, rocking forward on his brogues, balding and loving it, the hotel manager and a pair of bus boys waiting to remove his bags. Showing him to his room, the manager promised Nige his vote. Kick em out, he says, and Nige responds with a non-committal smile.

Nige feels woozy from his lunchtime boozing. It's never suited him, ale; he found Brussels a welcome break from his frankly distasteful diet of pies, cake and ale. The European diet suits his stomach. Wine, pasta: his temperament is soothed by the fish, too. Instead, he battles through pork and hops, with each gulp wishing he was sun-flecked in Cannes, paddling with his trouser legs rolled up in the crystal Aegean, sipped an espresso and breaking a cannoli whilst watching the Italian girls on their bicycles in Rome. He classed his diet, driving him, no doubt, to an early grave, as his sacrifice for the struggle for fiscal independence from the EUSSR. He removes his trousers as soon as he's in the room.

— I need a nap, Melissa

His sleep is fitful; he feels the sausages from lunch pushing against his bladder, tipping over the edge with hoppy, rich urine. Jesus Christ, he thinks: this country's cuisine. Why fight for it? He dreams of victory over the LIBLAB-CONS, he dreams of pretty French girls, he dreams of a decent coffee, he dreams of a quiet glory, a farmhouse in the South of France. He rolls over, he farts, he dreads dinner with the lifeless dullards that comprise the Gannet North bourgeoisie. He wakes with the lines of the sheet pressed into his face, and a sad dread. When did he sign up for this? When did life become a public performance like this? Pulling on his slacks, he grabs his fags from the bedside table and walks towards the balcony door. He catches himself in the mirror. Christ, I need something to pep me up, he thinks. I need a shave, a need a chance. I need some decent conversation for once. This is my life from now on, if I win. This is the life of an MP; a carousel of anomie. He pushes his finger up against his eyeball.

Shaking his jowls, he cracks open the balcony door an inch. Good, the door isn't overlooked. He fastens his flies, opens the door a foot, and takes a good look around. The hotel manager had sorted him out here; tall trees shrouded the side garden. He lights a fag, draws deeply, and exhales.

At dinner, temporarily revived with a cheeky pastis supped in his locked en-suite bathroom, paid for in cash from the Polish busboy, Nige pulls his body up from his seat to address the room. He takes a deep sup of the English wine on his table, accepting the applause of the assembled. He sees a sea of picked out white pinheads, throttled at the next in ecclesiastical purple ties, gold handkerchiefs pushed into the upper pockets. A young woman has slid his half-finished dinner plate from under his nose. Pork again. On his feet, he clears his throat.

The crowd lap up his words; his attack on the vested interests of the metropolitan elite, the out-of-touch euronazis in Westminster, the

Tories who have betrayed their party, the PC thugs of Zanu-Liebore, is echoed back to him in cheers and applause. He rails against the gravy train bureaucrats:

— Gannet is our chance!

He bellows

— Our chance to give the Tories a bloody nose! To put an end to the rule by dictat of the Brussels mafia! To bring power back to the people of the United Kingdom. Vote UKIP for national sovereignty!

He raises his glass as the room erupts. The floor rumbles with the scraping of chairs as the assembled bozos and pinheads rise to their feet. The Mayor's wife, thanked so effusively at the opening of Nige's demagogic volley, glows visibly with pride at the gushing audience, her role as the midwife of middle-brow secured in the town for a decade more. At the back of the room, Nige catches the eye of someone stood, but not clapping; her clothes mark her out from the two-piece women. She stands broadly, her shoulders pinned back, and she's swaddled in snug, utilitarian wear. He finds his eyes immediately drawn to her hair, pinned behind her head in a tight bun. This is a woman who can crack walnuts, he thought. What a pleasant change; his mind lost suddenly in a reverie. Is this a dream?

Most of the guests have left by the time Nige finally manages to get a proper drink from the member's bar. He gazes over the head of a local councilor, ignoring his tedious musings on the need for a new crusade, to glance around the room. The stuffed tench, the framed picture of the HMS Victory, the brass signs pointing to the gents, the stunning Valkyrie propping up the bar, picking pork from her teeth with a gold-handled flick knife, the aging taxidermied stag, fraying around the mouth...

Wait a second

... the Valkyrie! The bronzed, blonde maiden who caught his eye from the dining room; not a fiction, not a reverie, but a flesh and blood amazon! Her eyes locked on him, and he was no more able to move than that monarch of the glen before his last breath. She traced his purple tie down the centre of his double-breasted suit, lingering a while on his crotch, before slowly dragging herself back to his gaze. The knife closed in her hand and she sank her drink.

His conversation with the Templar dropped off, and, making his excuses, he left to walk over to her. She had already reached him, and thrust her hand into his.

– Mr Farage

her voice betrayed a crystal upper-class accent, tinged with the continent; not German, but Austrian, perhaps, he thought.

– I was impressed with your speech. Very impressed. I would like to discuss it further with you, in private, if we may.

The bar was emptying of stragglers from the talk, most well lubricated. He eyed a snug in the corner of the room, and she gestured to it.

– My name is Gutrot Essenem. I drove here from London tonight, to see you. I have booked a room in this hotel. I am a big fan of yours

Nige blushed pink

– Please forgive me; would you like another drink?

Gutrot reminded Nige of the women he knew from Brussels; charming, well read, with a hint of something exotic about them. Whilst a serving MEP he would turn his back on the

EU anthem, and watch the women of Europe's major political parties, hands to their breasts, and stare in awe at them. Gutrot was no different; whilst she didn't hold the same views as Nige, she took him at his word. Before he knew what had happened, 2 hours had been lost in often-ferocious argument, with well wishers turned away, until finally the barman came over.

– I'm sorry, Mr Farage, but I really must be closing the bar now. If you'd like, I can have drinks sent to your room?

Nige checked his watch

– My gosh, I'm sorry there, time really has slipped passed me

he replied

– Gutrot, perhaps we should call it a night

– Well perhaps, Mr Farage

– Please, call me Nigel

– Nigel

– perhaps we could take one more for the road? I really would like your opinion on future Common Agricultural Policy

Nige glanced again at his watch, then to Gutrot, then thought of his wife back in Surrey…

— Well, I'd hate to be seen as impolite

   he turned to the barman
— can we have the same again, to take into the lounge?
— Certainly Mr Farage

   the barman turned on his heel.

As the bar was closed, Nige and Gutrot continued on the vagaries of the CAP, but Nige felt Gutrot's eyes wandering. Perhaps he had been a fool to be swayed by her young charms, he though, as he watched her watch the barman, young, slim, adventurous - everything he wanted to be, and no longer was. He felt the whisky push back into his nose. There's no fool like an old fool, he thought; what would a beautiful young lady like Gutrot want with someone like me, a pasty-faced Englishman, a blimp, more pork than man. He lowered his eyes to the floor. A wasted evening, he thought, and my own fault. But as he raised his eyes, he saw she'd watched the barman leave the room, and was now leaning forward on her seat, close enough to kiss him.

— Nigel

   she said

— are you naughty?

Nige thought of his wife again. God, could he go through with this? What if this was a sting? But what if he didn't take this chance; what if he was condemned to be a sexless MP forever, far away from his beloved Brussels, chaste in Gannet? God, Nige, get a grip, you only live once...

— Well perhaps some people might say I have a fruity side

He chortled to himself. If only Godders could see him now, he thought! He'd take back those nasty things he said about me, about my john Thomas, when I chucked him out. He'd regret calling me frigid. Fuck Godders, I'm in.

— Then follow me

On her feet, Gutrot towered over Nige. She offered him a hand to get up, and he counted the 6 rings on her fingers; the cross, the skull, the circled A. Who was this woman? A biker? A commie? A witch?

As they walked through the hall, Nige turned to walk the stairs. But Gutrot gripped his hand tighter, too tightly, and pulled his arm too firmly too, and dragged him past the stairwell towards a door marked "Staff Only". She cracked the door a little, and, checking the coast was clear, pulled Nige through. It was dark, and chilly. The clammy cold clung to Nige's skin. He felt a little sweaty with nerves, and brushed his hair aside, once, twice, across his forehead. In the dark, Gutrot fumbled for the light switch. Illuminated, they found themselves at the top of a steep stairwell to a basement. Gutrot's hair was closed enough to smell; a citrus, pine, smoky smell, like Napoleon's stables on campaign, like the catacombs of Paris, like the bedchamber of Frederick the Great. She turned, and their faces were up against each other; her wrinkled button nose, her fine eyebrows, he traced them in his mind, never to forget, as she traced his outline, his droopy-dawg grin waking into a broad smile. This wasn't pork. This was so far from pork that he couldn't even think about pork. He could just think about her, her body, his rage to touch her skin. As he lent in to kiss her, she gripped his hand, then let go.

— Come, Nigel

and began her trot down towards the darkened cellar. He sighed, deeply, as he watched her disappear into the damp blackness.

When he reach the bottom of the stairs, he felt a hanging light cord playing around his ears. Pulling it, the beer cellar appeared in front of him; the metal casks, with tubes running up beneath the floorboards overhead. The discarded empties in blue plastic bins. And, before him, Gutrot, perched atop crates of Spitfire ale, slowly unzipping her tight polyester sportswear top to reveal a perfect cleavage. Nige felt his dick twitch a little, felt 20 years younger, felt the way he felt at Dulwich when he sang those songs to impress girls, swinging his marching arms. This was what he signed up for, he thought - the life of a soldier, girls, honour, distinction. A cut above.

Her zipping stopped. She looked up from her breasts into Nigel's eyes, watching sweat droplets forming on his forehead. Dropping the zipper, she pushed a finger into her cleavage, hooping around a necklace, drawing something out. Nige gulped. She grinned, and pulled up a silver encasement around a small brown vial.

– Do you, Nigel?

She asked

– Do I... do I what?

He gulped, feeling a stickiness around his collar

– Do you indulge? Do you... get high?

This is it, he thought. He glanced around the room, looking for something, anything, to indicate the trap: a photographer, a microphone.

– Is this a trap? I don't do cocaine, Gutrot

He stuttered

– Cocaine?

She let out a single, staccato laugh

– No, Nigel, I do not do cocaine either. This something a little more wild, a little more fun. Besides, cocaine tends to... how to you say... affect my prowess

The word appeared to purr out of her mouth

– Then what's in the bottle?

He asked

– Oh this?

Gutrot popped the vial from its casing, which, Nigel could now see, was a tiny replica of the EU parliament building, wrapped around the brown glass

— This is just a little something I picked up in Brussels. It's nothing illegal, trust me!

She giggled

— At least... not under EU law...

One eyebrow lifted and her mouth gave an alluring half-smile the likes of which he hadn't seen since that wild, unforgivable afternoon with Glenys Kinnock. He closed his eyes, as if about to jump into the icy North Sea that lay at the bottom of the country house hotel's garden.

— Well

He offered

— I might as well take the opportunity whilst I have the chance!

And moved over to the stacked crates of ale. Gutrot's thin fingers carefully unscrewed the lid, and swiftly she popped a thumb over the tiny bottle's opening.

Gutrot held Nige's face softly under the chin, turning it to face her. He could feel her sweet apple-breath against his skin; no, not pork. He closed his eyes and could almost feel it as the warm wind of the Algarve, with orange blossom from the orchards drifting across his sandaled feet. For a second, he was 1000 miles away from Gannet North, amongst the sweet, earthly caress of the Schengen Zone, where his soul could rest at peace. He felt her hand run over his cheek. Who was this maiden, he thought? Suddenly, she gripped his nose in a pinch, between thumb and forefinger. His eyes opened to her. She had pushed the bottle up to his nostril; he could feel the glass was warm from her breast.

— Now, Nigel

She whispered, careful not to alert the staff on night-duty above

— Nigel, I want you to take a deep breath through your nose

as she let her thumb off the side of his nose. Nige huffed. Not a sniffle of an old lady diligently making her way to the ballot box in the rain, despite an oncoming cold. Not the side-sniff of a newspaper editor of a conservative magazine after one too many lines. No, a deep, manly British huff, filling his throat and lungs with the vapor that escaped the bottle like a genie, bringing its magic wishes to his blood vessels.

He felt his pupils expand. Air rushed into his mind, clearing out the cobwebs; blood rushed through his body. His guts felt lightened, momentarily empty of the pork that stubbornly lined his colon. For a second, he felt paradise in this woman's touch; the weariness of life on the campaign trail dropped away, the monotonous conversations about immigrants and asylum seekers, the wittering nonsenses of people who described themselves as hard-working family, the whole charade his work life, a burden he had felt he might carry forever, disappeared. For a short few minutes, he was carried in the air away from the Bovril and Union Jacks and Gollywogs to a wheat field far away, picnicking on soft cheese and rich cured sausage; his popping ears echoed like prosecco corks. He felt his muscles relax; he felt his nipples brush against the inside of his shirt, his neck throbbing where just hours earlier it had been strung shut with his tie. A moment of chemical paradise ran through him as the softness of this pure woman, Gutrot Essenem, divinity, his angel.

– Good gosh

He exclaimed, as he finally caught a breath

– Good god woman, I feel... I feel so free. What... what is that?

Gutrot was screwing the bottle shut, sniffing back her shot. She turned to him, running her hand along the side of her head.

– Nigel

she said

– Does it matter?

– That was the most incredible feeling I've ever had. How can I get those? What are they?

Gutrot sniffed deeply.

– Nigel, I have a confession. I have misled you.

Her admission barely seemed to register with Nige, so blissed out on the crates of Spitfire was he.

– Nigel, these... these are poppers.

– My god

Nige said, sitting up with a start.

– Well... that's not a problem, is it? As far as I'm aware, that's ok. I'm not going to jail for poppers, am I?

His tongue was shooting off ahead of him now

– Well Nigel... this is why I came for you. I need you help. I need you...

Her eyes no longer had those silky Belgian charms. Flushed with joy, in her sad, puppy-dog eyes Nige could see the sorrows of all Europe.

— How can I help?

His concern wasn't entirely selfless. Sure, he felt deeply for whatever it was that had caused such sorry in such a goddess, but damn, he needed another fix. He watched the encased vial dropping down her cleavage. Suddenly it felt an impenetrable chasm, trapping his only chance at true joy out of his reach. He felt his head grow heavy, tingle, hurt.

— Nigel. I must confide in you. Whilst I don't agree with the majority of your policies, which, frankly, I regard as cheap demagoguery appealing to reactionary, barely disguised racism of the British middle-class, you are the only one who can help me. Our fates are intertwined in your success or failure...

She looked so helpless now, he almost regretted his base desires just minutes earlier.

— I work hard, Nigel. I am an honest, kind, law-abiding person. But I have one weakness. For years poppers have been a source of great joy for me; in a world of struggle and hardship, poppers offer me relief, pleasure... poppers are the flesh of my life, Nigel. But today, I cannot find this joy any more. Today, poppers are usually synthetic approximations of the original compound, amyl nitrite (isoamyl nitrite, isopentyl nitrite), cyclohexyl nitrite, and isopropyl nitrite (2-propyl nitrite). But that is a charade! A chemical farce! What I gave you - that's the good stuff: isobutyl nitrite (2-methylpropyl nitrite). Yes, perhaps what I did was wrong, to mislead you, but I am a desperate woman! We figured the only way we could return to a world where honest, hard-working men and women could freely buy genuine poppers without fear of arrest or persecution by the EUSSR brownshirts was if someone, somewhere in Europe was elected under the premise of dismantling the tyranny of the fascist-communist EU, and could repeal Directive 2005/90/EC of the European Parliament and of the Council. I am here to help you, Nigel

– but please, return isobutyl nitrite to the children of liberty!

CHAPTER 5

I tap my fingers in a counterclockwise direction tap tap tap tap opposite direction of travel to the rainbow spinning wheel of death tap tap tap tap like spinners on car wheels tap tap tap tap and it's loading actually it's finished it finished whilst I drained this coffee and slammed it down thinking "frustration" but then you'd know all about that what with you having the same log-on process of email then social networks if you're feeling playful or vice-versa if you've kidded yourself into thinking you're going to do some work or business other than trawling a cock ranking a database of self-shots in dirty bathroom mirrors which tends to be the end result of my log-in routine. What's yours? Owen? What browser do you open? What draws you in first? I find if I'm expecting good news I'm straight into gmail. I wonder what your quirks are? I'll save your blushes a little here but sites to find my hole on feature sharp in my routine. I think about you stumbling on my profile, about your browsing environment, and wait for you to turn up. Where the fuck is this man. I tap tap tap on the table and suck a cold one through the straw. You're on time, and you know how to talk.

— You're good

you said, on our first proper date as you rose from your seat to head to the toilet. It wasn't much but it was the indication that you were just a little shy, but in your mind you (too) wanted just a sordid fuck up. When you'd walked in you'd placed a hand in the small of my back, just above the buttocks.

— What can I get you?

I'd finished my coke, and was chasing the ice round the bottom of my glass with the straw. I specifically ordered something with a mixer, as I'd seen your eyes browse the beer taps. I was in no mood to embarrass you by forgetting my lines; we knew how this encounter was supposed to go, even if, on your profile, you'd been too savvy to write "straight-acting". So I had something with a mixer, you ordered a beer and I made a wager with myself as to how many pints I'd have to sit through for the charade to have its magical effect. Three, I was feeling lucky. And you'd be bloated.

— How's work

We hadn't discussed my job before. I'd just come to the end of a three-month short contract doing Christmas stuff in a call centre near Farringdon. Now that was over I was signing on again, but how do you bring that into conversation? Raising it now would be like spreading that loathing and disgust into all parts of my life. I have no reason to do that.

— Good. Just some admin stuff

The night juddered along in conversation a bit like that, but fizzed at the sight of each other. I leant forward and played with my drink and you leant back, thumb hooked through your belt loop.

It was fun and that, but I dunno, it felt a bit bait doing this thing where I was this girl you bought drinks for and the fact I had a dick was just this inconvenience idk

— So, do you meet up with many guys from grindr

Owen asked, his eyes flicking up into a mischievous little titter. He lifted his beer to his mouth, and his lips moistened as he waited for me answer

— I guess so. I don't often go on dates with

them though

— Don't you feel it devalues meeting guys tho? I mean is this the way we're supposed to really conduct ourselves?

What a tedious question

— what's wrong about knowing what you want?

He pushed the half-cut lager to the extent of his arm

— I dunno. I mean, obviously I don't have a problem with it, I just think maybe this culture is just because we can't be normal you know. It's hardly romantic

I spewed into my mouth at the thought

— Romance is a fucking bozo idea. I like touching people up; I decide what I want from people I fuck. If you want romance, go it for

He was trying to hold his nervous smile

— But I want skin and spit and dick

I gulped myself at playing a risky hand with this tight-arsed motherfucker. If I didn't know those nipples I wouldn't have bothered but I did so I was.

I felt bad immediately. The boy wanted the role-play, takes all sorts, takes all sorts to get some men hard. Some men can't just fuck-and-go and the little fake romance was something I'd tolerate, I thought, as the smiley barmaid, all teeth and tits and swishy, horsey ponytail, cleared out empties. I wasn't doing anything and I think you bought all my drinks b/c you presumed felt that was a top's duty. Your company was good, though; don't get me wrong; you were smart and cute, just cripplingly social.

I was touched you wanted to think about me this way, even if you wanting to think about it was more than me actually giving you those thoughts. It was removed from being a necessity. I'd already seen your cock (you sent it in your second message, sent 1:08am, you had finished work late and needed something as a nightcap. Decapitated pretty viciously at C4 on the vertebral column, but wearing the same shirt as in your profile photo, evidently taken months before with work colleagues to whom you were a dislocated acquaintance). But I liked that; not so much goods on the table, but rather a shared secret kept between us two in within the four walls of this All Bar One.

It had shorn the flirting into its constituent

parts - the practicality of getting me fucked and the drinks, and the cautious under-table nudges, and this fear that spread across your face and made you more evidently homosexual than even drinking with a faggot ever could. You covered your discomfort badly, always catching yourself enjoying yourself and pulling your body into a totally masc and awkward position. All because you'd not yet developed a social process where you'd just feel comfortable getting onto me into me or me into you. How I played this would, I felt, dictate the theatrics of the night's fuck.

That morning I'd arrived in Farringdon at a featureless, toothless office block, for an interview for another data entry job. I fucked up the interview with some stumbling answers. I'd had a little experience before but I could tell I wasn't the first choice. It wasn't my first choice but then I never get my first choice; being able to define it would help realise it, but I'd never seen it so how could I describe it?
— So, do you enjoy your job

Owen asked. I thought back to my last one. I role-played myself a little.

— Oh, you know. There's some nice people in my office, but the work's pretty boring like.

I think about looking around my office, about the little mental map of where I get fun and where I get shit. I got my shifts a day or two in advance, and spent them doing something slightly above menial data-labour: it wasn't just filling in spreadsheets; there was some element of interpretation of in there, enough that I couldn't drift off but not enough to stimulate me, not vaguely.

— I feed in the information, processed, and run it through algorithms.

— And what do you actually do?

— Actually I don't work there any more

— Oh right I thought

— Yeah no I just didn't want to say

— That's ok

— There's not much to say. Work was consistent. It came with a strange pace depending on targets, on the pressure line managers were under.

Days started fast, but as the morning ran on we paced ourselves.

We had an hourly target, which resulted in deductions if we failed to meet it; or unpaid overtime to catch up. Same difference. Unless someone on the team fucked up, though, reaching the target was easy. Bonuses began when we hit an arbitrary target above the standard day rate

— say, 5%.

— That's interesting

— Is it? We regulated the amount of times we achieved bonus; it became a pacesetter, a new target to be reached, and the standard went up. It only goes up. It never goes down. I never met the people who devised those algorithms, though. We fed information into our algorithm, and in turn our feeding was fed into another algorithm. It's algorithms all the way down.

Owen leant forward a little.

— What does that mean?

— It means I realised a long time ago these algorithms rule my life, make these decisions for me, and the way I live online, and in this city.

— I get you; the information keeps coming and there's some sort of pattern but you can't figure it out. It's too fast. Too much bullshit; I know that. I know the aggression. Don't think I don't.

You should see what I put up with every day
— I'm not talking about that. I mean they're
godlike. And I'm not scared by them, I'm not
mad at them any more. I just want them to work
better. They structure everything - buildings
don't work without them these days. Organi-
sations fit together in ways humans can't read,
only machines. I've given up resisting now.
— Resisting what? All these stimulants.
— No, I want stimulants. I want the algorithms.
I just want them to deliver the promises they
implicitly made. I'm happy to live in the filter
bubble, but why won't it deliver what I need?
— What do you need?

I looked at the table, through the table,
through the blue denim, through the H&M
underwear, through to a penis I could tell was
swelling as we got boozier and as I rolled my
t-shirt sleeves up so his eyes caught my arms and
ran up to beneath my arm pit and he thought
about my hard little nipples. Kiss me, Owen.
Kiss me amongst the England flags, fluttering
from the balconies. Let me brush away the hair
from your soft pale face, let my lips touch yours,
let me grab your dick on the nightbus

I thought

— I realized about 3 months ago that I enjoy the mediation of experience. Some might say, I don't know, that it means I'm not really experiencing it, but isn't that just the crankiest position you've ever heard? That sounds like someone living in the past. I like the control, I like the disinvestment. I like getting the burst of information I want, when I want it, with the ability to turn it off. Life is better without risk. Why does no one ever put across my side of the story?

He looked across at me

— And what about me? What about my side of the story?

— What about your side?

— Who speaks for my control, my lack of control? Who makes sure I get what I need?

— What do you need?

I'm drunk. I was drunk by the time we get down to it. I'm not checking my apps, shit, I'm not even sure where I put my phone. I grab onto his arm as we jump off the bus and feel him shiver, at my touch lol. I log on as Owen undresses me. I dream in drop-down menus, so it's easy for me to imagine. I'm teasing him with my tight apparel. The jeans unmistakably broadcast it and that's unmistakably a bead of sweat running from his forehead. I bought them 4 yrs ago and I've gotten fatter around the arse since then. My arse is too round, and my top half is no easier for him. But I'm ticking his checkbox baby. I'm a UI that's just totally intuitive. There's no gap for air between my shirt and chest. The skin is there and the collar is cut to a V and I'm pinched. I swing my hip out, I'm teasing, and he hates to be seen with me like this. He knows where to touch me.

I find myself on my knees and there's this bristle thing going on as I sink myself down. Eyelashes became important as thick highlights to the whites of my eyes. Grooming, that's important here - a fresh haircut and stubble. In this situation I check a number of things — curvature of the spine, the contrast of flesh and fabric, and ephemera in the room. Empty Bollinger bottle, television, things hanging on the backs of doors. I could hear thudding from his flatmates fucking, I felt queasy and he felt violent.

We'd drunk too much. The sex was bullshit, to be honest, and we knew it. He looked exhausted before we began. Not that it wasn't a performance. His dick kept slipping out of me. We didn't kiss enough. He fucked my arse in a way that suggested he wanted it over with because he wanted it too much, and I was bored and he ended by falling into me more frustrated than he began. I didn't cum.

I had fitful sleep, the way you do when you're sleeping with someone new, but I was dehydrated too. I was slipping in and out of a drunken delirium. I turned, close to slipping off the side of the bed, shifting myself back into a more comfortable place. As he lay his hands on me, all I could think was "I wish this were mediated". "I wish this was data"

I decided, then and there, that I want an algorithm to help me achieve better sex. I want to crave live sex more than mediated sex. I want it to be as perfect as when they do it. I decided, then and there, that I'd take any chance I was given to escape how I live, not robbing-desperate, but dead-behind-the-eyes-desperate. I decided there wasn't enough in my life to save, not compared. That night was really when my summer began; when I decided to take part in whatever came along.

Well, I've had a number of dead lovers. Not just dead. Expired. Owen's death was the first I would have had a hand in, though, politically speaking. It was a coincidence that one of the first fatalities of our new power was someone I'd already allowed into me, but I inscribed it as a sacrifice, as a part of the deal; sometimes decisions gotta be made, eggs gotta get broke.

CHAPTER 6

Owen was unbuttoning his shirt in the lift, top two plastic pearly buttons pushed through a field of blue checks.

— I thought it might be fun, you know...

He said, running his hand to my arse

— I always find hotel rooms sexy. I stay in them a lot, you know, all over the country. I travel for work, giving talks and stuff

— Yeah it is hot

I bit my lip in his direction.

He found the hotel keycard and let me into his room, dropping his shirt from his shoulders. He folded it neatly, laying it across the back of his chair.

— I was on TV earlier, did you see me?

— Oh, no, what channel?

— BBC 1, the Daily Politics

— I'd never seen it. I don't watch tv much

— It's terrifying what's happening to our country, Andy. I was up against Farage, at last. He's really capitalising on UKIP gains. I think Labour is underestimating them. I've been strategizing with the Labour Representation Committee about the possibility for mobilizing a sort of progressive patriotism at the next elections, in an attempt to undermine this anti-establishment, nationalistic vibe but what if it's too late?

He went on. I felt a dumb bond with him for a moment, as he struggled with his jeans around his ankles, telling me about accessibility, telling me about audience, talking to me as I lay back on these thick white sheets and opened my legs and shuddered. I felt sick, white sick. He lay his blue jeans neatly over his shirt; as I focused on it, the blue check that ran from collar to navel began to send me into a spin. Each square studded the fabric like a city block, with baby blue streets careering straight from nipple to ball sack. I could have lived in it, each check brushing daily against his body, telling it's own story of his flesh as he moved up and down the country meeting community activists and trade unionists. I felt the vodka running up the sides of my stomach. Blood flushed back and forth from body part to body part, making me first flush then go white. I had his body and my bills in my head, I had the boss in my head, I had this impotent anger and this hot, red skin on me, a thirst, a bad thirst for something more, for cooling water and for control again, power.

I lay on the bed and looked up to the ceiling. Turning over I grabbed a pile of magazines. The faces were unfamiliar, white, and Owen's voice failed to make words to me; instead just faces, ugly faces, and the blood disappearing from my face. A hand fell down to my arse, sliding from one cheek to the other and that jitter of fear caused my anus to clench tight shut, like I could guillotine off his finger, or constrict around him.

I felt the train I arrived on continue its rumbling inside me; my shivers were somehow scary now, not to me, but potentially scary, to him, if he felt what I felt, like he would push a finger up my ass, and think he could feel inside me, just like that. And those shivers would grab at his finger, and he'd shiver too, and my arsehole would slam shut, not slicing his finger, not drawing blood, but gripping it, tight and tight and tight till it was blue and I'd shove my ass in the air, a big round butt pushing up at him, a hungry bottom, slutty for his fingers, but he'd panic, a momentary panic everyone gets when

63

a finger and a hole create a vacuum. But this time the panic wouldn't subside; he'd try and use another finger to break the vacuum, free his finger from rectum which just a minute ago he couldn't wait to feel inside, feel that warmth of inside-flesh, and he'd run the finger round the hot puckered ring and spit on me, spit between my rolling, bouncing ass cheeks and let his mucus dribble toward his finger trapped in my hole, my non-hole, and his chest flushes red and dappled and his face drains white but this is gonna be fine, just fine he thinks and he goes for it and tries to gape my anus with a third bony little finger and he feels it open a touch and he slides it in and I feel a rush of the cold air of the room filling my arsehole, making my guts gasp and I turn to look at him as he smiles with relief and I roll my eyes feeling him fingerfuck me and it feels good and he sneers at me, sneers like a fucking cop. Every man is a potential policeman.

And my arsehole snaps tight again, tighter this time, like a heavy tesco bag, cutting at the blood that pumped around his hand as he ran his fingers along inside me.

His face is still bloodless and he's breathing deeper and deeper, and his dick is filling his trackies. He's not talking now. The tip of his fat dick is pushing hard against his leg and tenting the grey cotton and with his free hand he grips it tight, pulls in, squeezes down it, rubbing along the length and pinching at his bell end, squeezing it out, and the grey goes darker at the tip, battleship not trackie, blooming out into a patch of wet precum soaked cotton, and I look back at him doing it and want to taste it. The next train is different. Louder, closer, a goods train, long and thundering and as I turn back to bury my face in the pillow I feel the rumble shake the cups from the desk, little cuplets of UHT bouncing with vibrations over the floor, shake the glass in the frame, swing the glass chandelier in the hallway, and my arsehole just grips tighter, and his panic is overtaken by that fat sweating cock pushed out between his legs.

I moan from the dick, up my front, and end with a grunt from my mouth. I pull my arms above me, over the pillow, gripping my own forearms, and push my head down, taking a deep breath as I feel him fingers struggling to escape my arse. He's a wriggler, fighting now, and the blood pumping through his hand runs right up against my skin, and I can feel his heartbeat inside me. I want to tell him my arse is not mine; I promised it to him, it has a mind of its own, it's wild, a wild and free-spirited rectum, but instead I just mutter this porny mmmmm, a lip-smacking, clear-heeled mmmmmmmm yeah boy and my arse, like a rabid dog, loosens its grip for a split second, just to get a better grip, and opens wide, wider still, dark inside and he's mesmerised and stops struggling, stop fucking struggling mate. He's transfixed for a second, eyes locked on my smooth form, my broad round shoulders pushed out, my rolling biceps running down, my gym-fit lateral muscles leading to my pinched back, arched like a slut, and this butt, this butt that has already caused such trouble, and his fingers, sitting there, above a toothless anus, a gummy arsehole, hoover-butt, wet and warm, and before he can pull out his two fingers it slams fast around his hand, his whole fucking hand, and he's beyond panic now, just horny, horny as all fuck, telling me how he wants his dick in me, and I breathe deep on these poppers that have rolled down the bed, a toxic deep inhale, and I'm horny too, hornier than him because this is happening to me.

My butt growls inside and sucks at his arm like spaghetti, sloppy spaghetti, my butt is a noisy eater and it pulls his arm tight, straining his shoulder blade. His face is flat white now, past pasty, a ghost, and his dick so big, pumping, I am sure I can see it pumping in his blue jeans, and the precum isn't just a patch now, but it's soaking him, his trousers sagging, waterlogged with sticky notjizz, hanging off his buttshelf, and with his free hand he pulled them down so I can see his cock hanging there. He uses the heel of one black leather shoe to kick the other off, then claws his toes on before collapse against the edge of the bed. This fat swinging cock just pours with sticky saliva and his eyes were rolling back into his head. His brow is buckled up, his hair sticking to the bloodless flesh wet with sweat, and my ass just chomps and chomps away, his elbow now half way in, and these fat ass cheeks turning clockwise and counterclockwise. I grip onto the sheets and shake my fists; I've never felt anything like this, my ass is magic, it makes my balls fizz and rivulets run over them, matting in my butt hair, tangling my pubes into long dreads, knotted and twisted with salty ass sweat and grebs of spittle. What the fuck is happening? The trains sound closer and closer; I can see the desk, rattling, walking itself across the floor in nods and jumps, its fake legs skating towards the wardrobe, the doors there rattling, a drilling buzz of coathangers sliding about the rail.

I look behind me and Owen's shoulder deep in my anus and I feel my pupils getting wider and wider. For a second I think fuck, he's lost consciousness

— babe? You good?

He throws his head from side to side, trying to bring himself around. His hand grabs around his knob, and by now it's thumping, 8 inches of hot wet flesh, and his eyes roll around his head, and he groans, jacking away at his dick. He's a semi-man, tugging away, ashen with flaming red balls, consumed, and all I can feel are these effervescent anal fireworks, a fizzing butt party, and the harder it pulls him the sluttier I feel, and god it feels amazing. I open my legs wider, thrust my chest to the bed, hoist my ass higher as it winches his collarbone up inside me, his neck twisted. He regains his senses, and pushes the fingers of his other hand into my ring. He's in a spunk-fuelled stupor, a high that pumps more an more opiatic pleasure into his balls, and he's grinning and his dick is pumping out spunk, not precum but thick white globules, a rhythmic pump pump pump, covering the bed, dribbling over my body, pooling in thick reservoirs on his chest and stomach, but even as this sense of purest bodily joy takes control he can see where this is going. He forces his hand into my ass, grabbing my ring and pulls to free himself, but we make eye contact and his panicked eyes look powerless now, pathetic, bordering on cute. His hand is stuck, his second hand, his free hand, and within moments his wrist has gone. Knees are pushed against the side of the bed but this throbbing ass turbine is too powerful, sucking him into my rectum, twisting and churning him.

It feels like the train is bearing down on us now, thousands of tonnes of goods and raw materials driven by a vast locomotive, the bedframe rumbling like rails. The noise is almost unbearable; the whole room seems to be shaking, thudding from side to side. My knees straddle the bed, the sheets torn from the mattress; my cock drips with the sweat running from this site of consummation, and inside I can feel my ass cavity churning up his flesh, pulling his fingers from sockets, crushing his wrists. His face is beyond serene, though. We look at each other in this breathless ecstasy - he seems so peaceful, knowing that this is it, this is the end of his brief time here, willing himself towards death in the warmth of my rectum, sweating semen from every pore. I try to talk to him, but he's gone now, to a better place; blood is returning to his face, and his stoned eyes flicker with comprehension. I bite my lip, I love the sleaze. He smiles at me, and in that moment I know he trusts me, he trusts my ass. It could do anything to him, anything at all, he's convinced. He smiles, and I smile, and he does it, he fucking does it, he forces his head between my legs. His hair bristles against my buttcheeks but there is no pain. Just pleasure, as my butt gulps him in, and I rock forwards and back, the greatest power bottom ever bred, a prizewinner, a destroyer of the penis.

The noise of the train is quieting, my butt is finishing the job, and within minutes he is pulled deep inside me, ingested, brewed, stewed by my ass till all that is left is his trousers trailing from my arsehole, his black socks coiled lifeless like used rubbers on the floor. I pant and breathe in victory, so proud of my heroic butthole. It plans its conquest. If I had my way it'd never stop. I'd let my anal juices, that seem to make my insides so desirable to all these ball havers, these swinging-totem poles, these bureaucrats and these penised shitehawks who insist on mouthbreathing round the city like little princes, I'd let my anal juices digest his skin and bones and all this fleshy matter like a flytrap, like a serpent. And now I've ingested Owen I don't want it to stop, I'd move onto the next man with my siren's buttocks, and one by one I'd suck them in and chew them up till one by one I'd hovered them all into my ever more

71

muscular rectal cavity and before I'd realized I've destroyed the male sex, destroyed them all, in their entirety, one by one, every man who writes and speaks and passes laws and checks documents and has an opinion, and I'd let this hot acidic anal syrup digest me from the insides and eat me up too so that no man survives, no more men, even myself, one by one, just to make sure.

I come to with a start as Owen shuts the bathroom door. I feel groggy from the booze, tired, and the hotel room looks just as I left it. My clothes still constrict me.

— hey boy

I look round as he kneels on the bed, both legs straddling mine. My pants are pulled down, my white briefs sticking up. The blue checked shirt is pulled straight over his head, his chest more defined than I thought. An unflattering cut to that jumper. He runs his hands across my butt, and his finger lingers over me twitching little arsehole. You're cutting in fine, I thought.

CHAPTER 7

Even in his fevered dreams, Nigel Farage hadn't expected a night like this. It was a PR stunt, an attempt to convince the electorate that UKIP were indeed a bona fide political party, two fingers up to the ratbags in Conservative Party HQ who still laughed behind Nige's back, who still made jokes at cocktail events about how "your protest vote will collapse now Boris is leader" and "there's no room on the right for a second party" and "only bumboys vote UKIP". Well, those fevered dreams had dissipated in the last 6 months, since that fateful meeting with Gutrot Essenem.

Ms Essenem had continued to make her weekly visits to Nige's office, under the auspices of negotiating an alliance between UKIP and the resurgent European right. The routine was the same; Gutrot arrived by black cab at 11am each Monday, carrying only a small documents file, and rang the doorbell at UKIP HQ in Marylebone. The black door would open, and Gutrot was directed to Melissa, who would usher her through the bustling corridors and up the stairwell to Nige's private study, located at the back of the building on the first floor. Nige's face would spread into a broad smile, teeth bared, at the sight of Gutrot, as she removed her black leather gloves and extended a hand to the leader.

Once Melissa had delivered their espresso's, concealed within the depths of a tea mug, and the door had slammed locked behind them, Farage would reach for his iPod, and scoot through to a suitable music. Usually Elgar, Vaughan Williams, some interminable English Pastoral: anything to mask their conversation from the microphones undoubtedly hidden around his office. By security services, by the EU, by party hardliners: who knew?

Their words distorted by the lilting Worcestershire melodies, they would embrace each other deeply. There was nothing sexual in Nigel and Gutrot's bond. Nige has discounted that the moment Gutrot had opened up to him a world of far more spiritual depth than mere sexual gratification. They had become something more than that, something approaching brothers, comrades. Comrade! Ahh, what a word! It was this, this sacred bond of struggle that Nige had been craving all these years! Not "gent", not "Englishman", not these solitary epithets; it was a title based on a relationship, based on this hard, secretive struggle, it was this he had craved, craved since his first comradely high marching beneath the flag during those heady Dulwich days. He realised his weeks now revolved around this Monday ritual, still thrilling to him even after all these months. Gutrot would lean back, take a good look at the man on whom all our hopes relied. Fate throws up such idiosyncratic men, she would think. Who would have thought the hopes of the party boys of Europe would lie with this strange little Englishman, with hair growing from his ears? Who would have thought salvation for rave girls across the continent would emerge in the figure clad in grey pinstripe? Who would have thought that pure sexual satisfaction for tight-arsed citizens of Europe would be delivered in the shape of a puffed-up, chain-smoking little bank manager like this?

Gutrot always took Nige's leather office chair, whilst Nige paced incessantly between door and window, peering into the rear garden, always jumpy, always watching.

— Relax, Nigel. No-one suspects. Our alibi is clear. And this cannot be traced

Gutrot would say, unzipping her top, fishing again between her cleavage for her EU Parliament, gurgling with pure relaxant joy.

— You must understand the risks, Ms Essenem. If I get outed now, the chances of legalisation die with me. I am the only hope for cutting Britain free of tyrannical popper-prohibition! Without me, these Tory traitors will only sell us further down the river to the bonkers bureaucrats and loony leftists in Euroland!

Gutrot paused, leaving the tiny parliament building swinging around her neckline. She would begin to lower it back between her knockers.

— Then perhaps... perhaps it would be better if you went without. Just until your victory arrives...

she would say

— No! Please, Gutrot, no! We're safe, I'm sure. I'm just worried... not about this! About something else... about... you know what the press are like in the UK! Even with Rupe batting for my team, you can't put a good scoop like this past them. But you are right... I'm worrying my little head over nothing...

Essenem extended her hand, the chain holding the delicious nectar swinging from her protruding index finger, tempting Nige from across the room.

– Good! Now, a little something for my English warrior...

Nige rushed across the room, snatching at the bottle bobbing above his desk

– Not all at once, Nigel!

His hands fumbled the little black lid as he fought to open it. The cracking sound of the child-safety lock, the smooth, lubricated twist... each sensation felt so warm to him, so comforting, as he lifted the little bottle to his nose, covered a nostril and gave a deep, relaxing, joyous huff...

– Oh... Oh god... oh god yes... YES

He dropped back into the red leather sofa in the corner of the room, head slumped back against the wall, illuminated by the picture lamp that shone on the framed portrait of Churchill above.

— Thank you, Gutrot. Thank you so much

Nige would lie there, knees pulled up to his chest, reveling in his slutty subjectivity for 30 minutes, occasionally clutching his forehead, whilst Gutrot Essenem looked over his plans, his upcoming itinerary. Gutrot was only here to give Nige his reward, to address his battle-plans. She never partook herself, not here. A clear rule for Gutrot: never get high on your own supply. Instead, she waited patiently for Nige to withdraw from his hazy stupor and return to the world.

Well, that battle-plan, with Gutrot's help, was more successful that Nige had ever expected. Yes, the decision to field a UKIP candidate in every constituency was a PR stunt, but the situation in Britain had changed. The political landscape was different now; the balmy summer had produced a self-confidence in the British middle-classes. A new series of The Darling Buds of May rejuvenated a lost passion for pride in the English countryside, even with the conspicuous absence of Pa Larkin. A trend for street-parties in newly-cleaned up central London boroughs had made UKIP's coffers flush with cash, as young white professionals sold home-made bunting to neighbours, whilst couples took up swing-dancing in ARP helmets. The Met Police had stepped up patrols in racially mixed neighbourhoods; the country was gripped by 1950's fever.

That fever, combined with the now-infamous One Show incident where it became clear that, contrary to popular opinion, Tory leader Boris Johnson really *couldn't* take a joke, had shifted the loyalties of the electorate. And here Nige stood, on this hot summer's evening, waiting for the count as the returning officer muttered inaudibly with his assistants in the Gannet Town Hall. The exit polls suggested that perhaps tonight something extraordinary was happening; a swing to UKIP that was sending shockwaves throughout the country. Perhaps this wasn't a landslide just yet, but heck, with the newly devolved powers to English MPs shaking up the electoral landscape, it looked like UKIP were sweeping the board across the country. Brian, now head of Nige's whole security operation, paced the hall nervously. Melissa fielded questions from an impatient press, just waiting to get a sound-bite from the party leader.

— Please, if you will just wait until after the count is declared, Mr Farage will, I assure you, give you all the quotes you'll need.

Painfully aware of the live TV coverage, Nige had boasted a rictus grin all night. Nevertheless, he was nervous. Very nervous. The pork pie and ale photo-shoot earlier in the afternoon had played merry havoc with his bowels. He longed for something light, a sfogliatella, like Pierre, the pastry chef at the European Parliament, used to make him. A glass of Italian rosé. Anything but the stodgy, heavy fruitcake delivered to him by an elderly supporter, which he dutifully washed down with tea from the enormous urn manned by the WI in the Town Hall count. He leaned over the Brian.

— I'm going for a fag, Brian.

Brian silently nodded his consent. He'd done a sweep of the rubbish area outside the back of the Town Hall designated a smoking area earlier in the evening.

Outside there was only a pimply young Labour Party researcher, drawing on a Malboro.

He'd been drafted in to help the Labour candidate's campaign. Realising the futility, he'd spent most of the night out here, smoking, and checking twitter. Occasionally he'd check his facebook, just to see the Tories he'd been to Oxford with just 2 years before gloating about UKIP victories across the country, most having dutifully defected earlier in the year after being promised plum positions as Special Advisors. Nige checked his pockets for his lighter. Bollocks, he must have dropped it during the meet-and-greet outside the count.

– Don't suppose you've got a light, by any chance?

Despite their differing loyalties, the young Labour researcher couldn't disguise being slightly star-struck to see the UKIP leader out here, alone in the dark, sticky night.

– Err, yes, of course

He responded, passing over the lighter to Nige

– You must be very pleased and excited

He enquired. Nige took a deep drag, then passed the lighter back. He spoke from behind a cloud of thick fag smoke.

— It's certainly going well for us, yes. I must say it's a little unexpected but we seem to have Bojo on the back foot.

He was jumping inside, if he was honest. The night seemed like a little miracle to him, as he looked up into the starry night, hearing the clanking of teacups from the women washing up in the kitchen inside, and the dull murmur of the assembled party apparatchiks and journalists inside the hall.

— And no major fuck-ups for the whole campaign!

The researcher offered. Nige shot him a side-eye glance

— Sorry... just, you know

Nige flicked his fag ash under the nearby metal wheelie bin

— I think we have sorted out a few hiccups in party discipline

He responded. The Labour bod looked no more than 15, to him, dressed up in a new suit with a red rosette pinned to his lapel.

— What about you

Nige asked

— Why are you here? Surely it's a waste of time.

Labour have never won Gannet North in its entire history. Shouldn't you be out pulling girls?

— I thought I'd see a campaign firsthand

The little twink responded

— Besides, the more no-hopers I attend, the quicker my own selection will come

Nige managed to withhold an eye-roll

— Hopefully not in a shithole like this though

He said

— No offence Nigel

— None taken.

The lad stubbed out his butt, stood for a second, then said

— well, guess I'll see you in there. Good luck

— Thanks. And you too, with your continued career.

As the door slammed, Nigel took a moment to contemplate the quiet. How had this happened? What decisions would he have to make from tomorrow? This should have been the greatest day of his political career, but instead, he pulled out the little brown bottle from his underpants and shook it, and felt despondent. Barely a hit left, he thought, and he hadn't seen

Gutrot Essenem for over a month. Not a phone call, and no way of contacting her. How would he ever find himself a new source for this liquid? He felt that he might wither without it; his campaign had been a masterstroke of political theatrics; he'd been firecracker throughout, winning a standing ovation at the televised leaders debate whilst an increasingly lost and disorientated Boris had ummed and ahhed, each joke falling more flat till he resorted to flagrant theft of Sid James one liners. Farage, on the other hand, sparkled with wit and panache, holding the corrupt Westminster elite and metropolitan apologists for Londonistan to account for their crimes. As the isobutyl nitrite (2-methylpropyl nitrite) flooded his body, his natural smile and effusive English charm flooded the nation's TV streams and twitter feeds. Even his natural enemies couldn't help but warm to the avuncular, down-to-earth stylistics.

But here he was, on the eve of the most important speech of his career, and he had only one hit of his potion left. Oh, whither the poppers queen, he thought, casting his eyes towards the heavens. A knock at the door, and Melissa's head appeared, and, with a stage whisper:

– Nigel! The returning officer is about to announce. You've got two minutes. Quickly, inside!

– Coming, Melissa. Just finishing this fag

– You're an addict, Nigel!

She replied, withdrawing to the yellow glow of the Town Hall. Nige laughed to himself. If only she knew, he thought, popping the top of his little bottle. With that, he huffed the last of his joy juice, dropped the bottle into the bin, and returned to the count.

CHAPTER 8

4 minutes from the tube station. The flats rose from the pavement 4 stories. It was greying wood, wreaked and streaky from dirty London rain. And the windows weren't symmetrical - they stuttered across the façade, punctuated by glass and steel balconies. Waiting for the lights to change, fiddling with the coins in my pocket, I looked 360 around me; the old boy with the dog waiting at the lights gave me a nod as I looked past him. His dog's mutty brown fur scuffed up against his collar as he fought with a ripped toy, his owner's attention elsewhere totally. Below my hookup's flats were a CHICKEN SHOP and a NEWSAGENTS. Squeezed onto the balcony, clothes horses, pressed silver and pink and black against the streets.

Travellers on passing buses were prurient; this was East London at its vibrant best, a fantastic mix of cultures living side-by-side with only residual human slaughter. In the window of the ESTATE AGENT, styled as a BAR for PERVERTS and MIDDLECLASS WANKERS there is a brightly lit LCD screen advocating the borough;-

"it is a very depressed place with all the noise and mess that the middle-class tourist takes for "vibrancy" but which could just as easily be desperation"

Right I said to myself, yeah I feel you. I'm stood in front of the glazing looking at the little computer people caught on photo walking across my neighbourhood. I'm trying to find myself, without luck. I must be here somewhere. Where's Wally. A hand slaps me broad across my shoulders, it's Pete, and it's been time. Pete works as a gardener, Pete's in an anarchist group up in Haringey, Pete's a twitchy animation.

– Chubz!

– Oh hey Pete

My hands are deep in my pocket, tossing a stinky copper coin between fingers, feeling the ridge of my briefs, toying my bell end. He looks at me looking at the little people.

He says

– they are bloody destroying this place

and he seats himself down on the ledge at the bottom of the window, as if his legs are linked to his body with an elastic band. The man is a walking banner as if to say yes he is part of your society but naw not in society as it were and he holds his with pride as well he might. I have seen him myself as a true Londoner and truely SCREAM as if to break apart the peace - YOU RICH FUCKING SCUMBAGE! - and threaten death upon people who are just going about their business and they think they are peaceable but my, they are not peaceable for, to Pete, their business is to DESTROY Pete. It makes sense for Pete to agitate strangers, because so much of his life is agitated by them and the world they've made easy on themselves. Pete tells me about his bail conditions, his upcoming court date. I tell him I'm off to get laid

— safe

he says.

I climb the flights of stairs to the correct number as indicated by his message. It is number 4. There is no mat outside, no children's boots or bike wheels, like outside the other flats. Number 5 is across the hall. Number 5 has a mat. It reads "Welcome to our Home" on it. I can smell cigarette smokes from number 5. The stairwell is quiet, and just before I ring the doorbell a noise pricks my ears.

Heavy breathing.

Scratching.

I pull up my trackies which were sagging and beginning to gather around my Lonsdales. The scratching is louder. I follow my ears; it is formless. But as I locate its source I can picture it. An image of it appears to me. It's coming from the foot of the door of number 5. It must be a dog, a small, aggressive dog. My worry turns to a snigger, and perhaps I should ring the bell of number 5. I rearrange my erection and get a touch of homesickness in my forehead.

In my mind I make a composite of Faron from the photos on his profile. How his head fits his body, how the skin from one photo, distorted through a dirty mirror, blends with the skin on his torso, bleached dry from the flash and the low voltage lighting of the gym shower rooms. He's a collage of iPhone shots, a frankenstein top I'm piecing together from bits of grindr and second-hand sensations.

I woke this morning with a sweaty judder, my smartphone littered with pornographic images of fat cocks still gripped and swelling from last night. My pants were tied up around

my ankles, I lay as I fell. I imagine it different-
ly where he wakes, virtually tucked in. The
room smells of carpet cleaner and lily-pollen.
Everything in its place; pictures framed, last
night's glass of water politely on the bedside
table. Smartphone on the bedside table charg-
ing and blinking, neat penis tucked into fresh
boxer shorts.. A defined line could be drawn
from tip-to-toe, a semi-erect penis (constant-
ly) fills a snug pouch, even precum drips in even
drops, just touching the brushed cotton and
resting there till it dissolves, filling a small air-
space with an essence, an essentially delicious
vapour of richness and sweetness.

Whatever happens, he cannot know how
much I would give to take that drop of him
alive on my tongue. I'm a different boy online,
I write out his fantasies, what he needs to hear
to bring me over. This is how I live. I project in
type the form he needs me to take. Each bright
red message betrays a new falsehood to him.

I get a particular thrill from sex organized
online. I measure the hookups in data involved,
uploaded or downloaded. I can trace the devel-
opment of our social tension and sexual thrill

through datestamps, and I can count them in bytes. I have never heard this mans voice. I have never seen his flesh bristle and twitch; every hint, insinuation, every targeted pause, I can account for as data. I never do. I never run the analysis. Quantifying is not the thrill. Disembodiment is the thrill, mediation, running desire through culture. Description, narrative. His hands are coded to his body, his body coded into flesh as the front door peels open.

His apartment reveals a desire for crispness and pressed form. There goes the greeting and he offers me a carlsberg and I take it. In his territory he can attend to things as a distraction - find a track, play it, disappear into the bedroom whilst I wait on a broad leather sofa, making a survey, balancing luxury electronics against sentimental keepsakes. We don't keep eye contact much; some guys hate that, I reckon.

I'm looking out his window, down onto the tops of buses, on top of the neighbouring shops with flat roofs picking up the brown leaves and crisp packets and plastic bags like a radio picking up static. Faron emerges with his top off. He's taller out of clothes, and broad. And dark, and his grooming is true with the pressed linen, the elasticated waistband crisp white. I run my hands around his waist, toned, not like mine, where my waistband pinches into warm fat. He kisses the side of my neck and my hands rise up his body, under his pits, and I can feel myself sinking, pulling off my t-shirt. I close my eyes and his body disappears, and the track changes again, and I can hear his ipod being put down, just as I arch my back down.

My knees hurt against his wooden floor. My knees distract me as his finger takes a route around my arsehole. He's dressed for the occasion; I can smell the peculiar air-conditioned tone on cotton of new underwear, the escalator grease of the shopping centre an integral ingredient of what is to follow, of what it is to follow. His hands rummage deep into my briefs, then pull out, slapping the elastic. He stands over me, and shifts his weight. The tension breaks as I feel his spit on my back, and my trousers slip from the arm of his sofa, spilling £3.70 in change across his new wooden floor.

In London, sadness rises like a smell from the sewers. This place isn't like that. Things are clear here, and, as a result, brighter. Here's the dynamic that runs between the two of us as we fuck. It's not the skin against fur. It's not the sensations of rough tongue running around the tip of his penis, licking under the head and balls and dipping into his hole. And it's not the weight of him pushing over me, lifting itself into my hips, though afterwards it's the weight that stays with me longer than the taste or smell; it's the sensation that lingers in muscle memory, like carrying heavy shopping then dumping it.

CHAPTER 9

Feet thudded and dropped to the platform before the train doors even opened fully. Chubz swung his body from the door and paused, checking back up and down the platform for the right exit. The platform swam with the first tide of commuters home, those who'd got out sharply, gone without a pint with workmates. Not trying to impress the boss. The crowd moved towards the thudding and slamming, thudding and slamming ticket gates. A station operative in a blue bib leant over the wide access gates, idly checking tickets for those who seek assistance.

– Well that's the problem

he said over his shoulder

– but if you report it nothing happens. I told em so many times

A policeman stood behind him, tucking both thumbs into a utility vest. His eyes scanned the crowd as he talked to the station manager

– Of course mate. Not in their interest

The gate thudded shut for Chubz and he slid his card over the reader and led forth with his shoulder past the cop and station manager. Running down the steps to the main atrium he skipped a step or two and swung round the corner.

Thud into two more feds.

— oh shit sorry

turning his way past them, and felt another thud immediately crack in his chest.

— wait a minute

"wait" being drawn out and Chubz closed his eyes in a silent curse against himself.

— In a rush mate? Come here

the thudded palm twisting into a fist that caught up a bunched t-shirt and pulled him against the wall. The dialogue was tediously unoriginal but he knew that you followed their script.

— why are you in such a rush mate?

his eyes followed the hi-vis up to the shirt collars, the fat neck of one, the tanned arterial of the other, the short stubble of a younger prick

— sorry?

The younger one said, right up in his face

— where are you off to in such a hurry?

The two had him in their zone of control -
every hand movement from a handbook of
pushing kids around in train stations.
— I'm visiting...
 he stuttered through
— I'm off to see a mate
 the concept seemed alien to the pasty one as
he leaned in and held Chubz shoulder
— and what's your name lad?
 his face was flabby, skin pushed up like
dough and his clothes seemed wedged on
around his cuffs
— Andy
— right Andy where are you off to in such a
hurry you can't show some manners?
 His thumb pushed into his shoulder blade
and Chubz smelt coffee on his breath. The
other one leant back and, with a single thumb,
wiped off the bead of sweat from behind his ear.
The ridge of his collar was stained.
 Chubz noted the exit felt farther away. The
two blokes holding him were cut as a silhouette
against a hazy vaseline light from the entrance
behind. The pavement beyond was baking in
the heat, it radiated, back, back into the cool

station concourse, and people cut across it as they walked along the street. A stench choked up his sinuses, of the fat one's coffee breath, stinking, and piss and samosas, and dusty dry cigarette ends and thermopaper receipts and stinking. Stinking.

– To see a friend.

Fuck it, these feds think I'm carrying or some shit, he thought.

– And where is this friend?

The stubbly one asked. He caught a glimpse of his watch as he shook out his shirt cuffs. 3/4 dials. Mark of a prick. A siren in the distance cut up the time.

– Err, up in Stoke Newington

– What's his name?

– Does it matter?

– If I ask it matters

And another siren coming closer.

The thought of all the commuters pulling past him. Everyone found their own way of dealing with this stinking heat, he thought. Everyone has their drink of choice. Their poison. He felt like this uniformed presence was a part of the commute. Authority likes to punch

into a crowd. Go fishing. Kick in doors, see
what they find.

— Owen. He's called Owen.

— Not so hard
    the pastry-faced one said

— come on

    pushing him into an alcove. The tide of
workers trickled out past them. There's such
a disconnect in this procedure. After so many
stop and searches the routine becomes tedious, not intimidating. You read through the
script to get out ASAP. There's a disconnect
between you and them as to where the intimidation lies. Each cop thinks himself uniquely
charismatic; intimidating and witty with it. He
thinks it's his patter that achieves acquiescence.
Every pig thinks himself something of a char-
acter. But they're not known for their people
skills. People with people skills don't become
cops. The attempts at intimidation or banter
are endured in an attempt to escape anything
approaching real conversation as quickly and
painlessly as possible. Say what they want to
hear. Chubz was suddenly aware he was alone
on the concourse.

— What does Owen do?

— I dunno bruv

His hand ran up my inner thigh. His gloved fingers felt like truncheons themselves, porky Kevlar flesh tubes pressing against my fresh cotton, and as I tried to close my legs he gripped me and raised his forearm. He leant in to me, close enough that his breathe felt stubbly against my lips, vinegary with deodorant, and a stench of greasy coffee. His hand gripped one of my shoulders, the length of his arms weighed against my chest and his elbow dug into my shoulder blade and he leant, right into me, cracking me like a knuckle.

— come on son

he whispered into my lips. His bulk was firm from body armour, warm and synthetic, and the opposite of what lay beneath, I thought, fleshy but cold and lifeless. I groped for the right response, the appropriate response to give to law, the truth as it appears to him.

— you must think I'm a mug

they write their own lines, cribbed from the shit heroics of the tv shows that first inspired them to serve their community

— what are you selling

I lifted my hand to his arm and his wasteman mate grabbed it

— stop fucking resisting!

he squeaks and his grip loosens on the flesh on my inner thigh, from a nip to a hold. I feel his fingers start to brush up and down, reaching where the tip of my dick hung, and he came in closer still

— are you gonna show me?

I felt surrounded by beard. I looked at the orange lcd ticker - 6 minutes. Wrong end of the concourse. Just not worth the struggle, I thought, as the two fingers formed a cup and sat beneath my balls. I heard a long rolling drumbeat approaching; a shit-splattered diesel train approached the station, a long train of coal hoppers passing through from port to power station.

He shoved. He shoved and shoved, a hand cupping my testicle, a freight train rushing through the station, hey mate, listen, a fat tongue hanging to his lips, a thumb running up the smooth worn warm cotton of my track-ies on the inside thigh.

He weighed on me; there was little movement. I rocked my shoulders, he pushed up as I tried to wriggle beneath this forearm. Painted pebbledash rubbed away against the back of my hoodie, stabbing through at my shoulder blades. The little fucker had made himself scarce, hidden behind the corner, hands and thumbs playing against the inside of his stabvest, and *I* want him stabbed, I want him shattered and fucking blood splattered on the floor, like a human again.

But here it was just me and this bulky fed. Quiet, almost. Quieter than usual in the city; no sirens, no shouting, no cars, and as the freight train rumbled its last through the platform, almost a serenity. And this dusty smell of the alcove I was in, where it was cold and opposite a cage of gas tanks. Fuck. Trapped. His hand was moving, flat-palmed, across my knob, up to where the fabric met my skin, my stomach. I tried to breathe deeply but his arm kept pushing the air out of me and every inbreath I could only smell him. He was looking down at what we was doing, then up at me - his eye caught the panic in mine, and he didn't smile, he looked as shocked as me for a split second, then we paused .

Then his palm flipped into a grip, twisted by his wrist he had my waistband I wanted to bite but he sprawled on me this grip on the waistband like a rope tightened around my waist my body was prepared that night for a fucking, for a joyful slutty fucking like I wanted this brutal assfucking I was on my way for and here this man stood and pushed up against me. His arms across my chest grabbed me and slammed me into the side of the alcove and for a brief second my lips touched this wet pebble-dash and a taste of iron and fungus hit the tip of my tongue and I felt my skin being scraped and grazed. And then my bell-end has pushed against it and my balls sucked up; the cunt had pulled down my pants and my arse was exposed to the warm breeze that carried the stenches of oil and brakefluid and fag smoke across the station. A body weight broader than mine pushed me into the corner and his hairy hand yanked my pants down to my thighs. From behind him all you could see was a dark corner, a black-clad bulk, a strip-search(?), and these two white ass cheeks and it looked funny, it would have looked funny if your train was passing through, and I tried to breathe again and I couldn't because now a whole man hand gripped my face. Two fingers broke off, two dirty fingers, entering the inside of my mouth where I was still wet where he was dry, and pulling against my cheek, and I could taste iron and salt and shit and I ran my tongue along his fingers because I wanted to do something, I wanted a say in what was happening.

Between my balls and arsehole his cupped hand rubbed against my skin. I'd made my asshole smooth for Owen, and now this man was feeling it. Kinda funny how you want to be owned, to give your holes for this other man to push things into, to please himself with, and here this man is doing that, and I don't know what to think. I guess I wanted the power of being owned, the power of being the hole. This man with this fatty rough flesh doesn't show me any respect. Doesn't let me let him own me. It's not even me he wants, he wants to own himself, he wants to be the big man. It's not about me, even as I feel his thumb running up against my smooth ring made smooth for a man who wants to run his thumb up me. I take a deep huff on his gross fat fingers, his dirty skin, and I feel his thumb, wide like a toe, a big toe, and hairy too, his dirty great hand-thumb push up into my rectum like a shite in reverse.

CHAPTER 10

Wind a fat dick round your little finger, feel a sweat like the dirty faggot you are, sweat sweat, not just a writhing hot sweat but an eyeballs crossed sickening cold one like a feather down the back I was shaking like this when the door swung open and out of this light hallway his hand reached out and held onto my forearm with all the deliberation of a priest.

Footsteps had a pace that triggered down the street; across this blazing portico a window slid shut as a disgruntled fitting. I itched
— hey come in
   I came in and
— hey hey so are you well
— yes yes
— you look a bit funny
— Nah just ill
— Maybe it's the weather
   not the fucking weather talk again I seem to always be talking about the weather and cum swapping. Shared house shoes had scuffed the wall and hung in a pile, badly piled, men and women worn out all on top of each other. The hall was warm and worn out. Framed posters

ran up the stairs, found. It was a thin terraced house, but nice. A smell came from the kitchen, and the housemates obviously knew each other.

— I've been thinking, Andy: do you want to get involved? You know, with the party? We need to organize a broad left consensus against the UKIPCONDEM coalition. I really think your personal skills could be useful at agitating local people in Bermondsey. Everyone seems to know you!

He thrust a leaflet in my hand, advertising a public meeting. Yeah I knew people, but not like he knew people. I stared at him; he must have read my blank expression.

— Just think about it, yeah?

— Yeah alright Owen. Alright.

As I passed his body he reached out. His hand cupped beneath my armpit, ran down my back, he could feel me quiver. I don't know how we manage to make

the call correctly, so often, between fear and arousal in our sex mates.

And there's a coffee smell and there's a bacon smell and I'd really like to throttle that fed cunt and we walk up the staircase. The feeling I intend you to get from all this is all very wooden floors and halogen lighting 4 years old but not too much. He was wearing socks and the room had the right lighting prepared and he was wearing trackies and a t-shirt I'd not seen him not in a shirt (except from the obvious you know).

– You look good

he remarked despite having just noted that I was fucking freaking out but. Thanks. But he looked good in the t-shirt. A sexy back is underrated that touch of flesh flashed between cotton is an underrated look too. All these suggest things to an open mind.

The night seemed to shine darker through the large squared panes than the bulb hanging back on the landing shined back out. The quiet of the back garden, a place extended since the start of the heat, overwhelmed the dirge of soft rock coming from his bedroom. You can smell the foxes. No stars tonight, just the cloud, bigger than earlier. Making the sky darker, in the early evening, a darkness we'd not seen all year, darkness in daytime. Maybe this is how the heat stops, I thought. This is new.

I thought I heard thunder but I thought again about the train line that ran from the station behind his house, down the embankment of brambles and ripped bedding and the shit that makes railway embankments so obscene. Probably a train with those pigs on it. Fuck those cunts. His arm lead back from a shoulder, bigger than you'd think. I held on to his little finger with my entire hand, and it made me skip those last few stairs. His door lay ahead, the floorboards ran straight in. He had prepared it for fucking. That made it teenage to me, cute, like we were swallowing cum before his parents got home.

He took a beer from his bedside table, cracked it, passed it to me.

— Thanks Owen

— What a day!

— Hmmm

I watched his thumbs, thin thumbs, push against the side of his tinny. We took a swig, I took a swig, I felt a yeasty fizz pushing up against my gums as I swilled my mouth. I could spit this on your floor right now, I thought. On you. Another swig, the cold beer running down my insides flooded my dry body, running down the cracks in my lips.

He was already pulling off his shirt, like a married man. I watched his sinewed hand lifting, revealing those button nips, pink with a quiver, and in my head this hairy pig hand up against my arsehole and nipping at me, nipping my ring. I thought of the policeman's head, and in my mind, ran through the process of crushing it between how I felt when I got on the train and how I feel now. The beer was starting to push bubbles through my mouth and tingle the bottom of my nose, and Owen was in his pants, a semi-hard cock lifting his boxers, his hands around my waist, and kissing at my neck

– come on, take these off

He said. Another order

– get on your knees, there's a good lad

I imagined what Owen would look like in body armour, in those broad Kevlar pads, what he'd look like leaning on a man, pushing his tented dick against a man in a train station. They're getting younger these days, young enough to suck a dick, fresh-faced. I imagine that's how Owen felt about me, like I was chaos, like I needed order. He looked young enough to be in school, young enough to be a copper, younger all the time to me. My tongue felt fat in my mouth and my eyes were stinging and I just did what he said, did what he said as he pulled his dick out, pushing his tip in through my lips and without a word grabbing the back of my head and thrusting forward. Unsteady, I slipped back against his bed, gagged on his cock, felt it wet with sticky salty precum by the time it hit the back of my throat. I thought about doing the same to the rough-handed policeman. I could see only his lips, with his truncheon being fed through like a piston, his head not resting against the cheap worn sheets of a Stokey bedroom but against the gravelly, gritty pebbledash of the station, and no fleshy warmth on the apparatus of the state apparatus, a black rubber taste as it hits the back of the coppers throat and just keeps going, hurting him, I'm filled with a desire suddenly, not for semen, not sexual, but retribution, violence, and I breathe deeply through my nose as Owen's dick pushes finally down my throat and saliva runs down chin.

The desire of him on me, for me, and my need to be on the copper, acting upon his body with mine with as much force but twice the power; it made his room shake. I don't know if he felt it but I felt the rumbling, like the streets had cracks and each house shook against the other, the whole street on the edge of collapse, weak. The windows didn't fit the frame; beneath my knees the gaps between the floorboards seemed to be wide enough to push a hand through, a crevice, and a toxic gas seemed to be leaking up. With each breath through my nose my eyes started to water more, red with anger, red faced. My knees were splayed across the floor, my trackies stretched. As I gagged down his cock he leant awkwardly over me to run his cotton soft hand down my arched back, his downy blond arm hair shivering across my shoulder blades, and a finger down my arse crack. I felt distressed, upset by the whole situation, unable to breath with this warm wet dick in my mouth, my buttcheeks pulling together thinking of that uniform, the clash of Owen's skin and the tanned leather of PC dickhead's thick sausagey fingers poking against my flesh, and I imagine taking them and breaking them at the knuckle, snapping like bamboo. Unable to get a finger inside me, he grabs me under my arms and lifts me onto the bed, dropping me and gripping my ankles in a move. Mouth is full of cotton, tongue is bleached dry. He grabs my trackie bottoms by my thighs, a bunch in each hand, and with one pull, my butt cheeks are exposed to the air, and I hear a rumble from the sky matching the sound of saliva gathering in the back of Owen's throat - a wet glob of phlegm aimed for my asshole, still hot and sore from the policeman's hand, aimed but missed, hitting the small of my back where my t-shirt has ridden up. The dribble down my side hits a nerve. My cock goes hard

— spit on me again

another gob hits the top of my arse crack, a rumble outside, the windows dark now, before sunset. A tongue running up from my bollocks, rough where my hair is growing out, and I pull my t-shirt off and feel his soothing tongue where earlier the train station wind was running

— fuck it

he reaches for the bedside table. Stiff runners stop the drawer from sliding and, one hand on my balls, he yanks the whole draw onto the floor. From his flies his dick is hanging out, hard and red. Notebooks, coins, scattered on the floor, from which he grabs a bottle of lube, red markings, and shakes. My face goes into the pillow and the cold liquid dribbles over my ass, and he rubs his fingers over it, slipping around my hole, and I imagine the coppers face right now, grinning to himself, already having had me. What if I'd punched him. Right then, with his thumb up me, just knocked three teeth out, pushed him back, off the platform, between the freight trucks of the train, losing his footing, pulled beneath the wheels, his body cut in two. What if then? Behind me Owen's teeth wrestle with a condom packet, and a minute later the tip of his dick hits my ring and I open and let him into me insides. His fingers grip my hips and he moans as soon as he slides, and I feel my ass filling into my belly, a sore power, and grunt with my exhale. He pulls back out, pushes back in, and I own this, I'm holding this cunts head under water, I'm turning the corner with my own private street gang. My head sinks further and further down towards the mattress and he speeds up; occasionally his dick drops out of my butt with a slurp, an interruption, and I shoot him a look

— ugh sorry

his face has flushed red and he looks as young as he ever does, and bright, concentrating hard, and he pushes back into me with a quiver and that's better, much better. His mouth starts up, his grunts form words that seem alien to his mouth

— baby

— fucking take that dick

his aggression changes my position, I arch up further and shake the trackies that are stuck on my ankle to the floor

— bitch

— little slut

— cocksuck...(inhale)...cocksucking...little...fag

He's pounding me hard and I think of that copper on the floor and I've got this bat in my hand, a baseball bat, he's tripped as he's run and I run to him and the moment I arrive, on instinct, I slam the bat down into his head and it slices through it, pure faggot retribution, pure sexual violence. I think about how he'd look at me, like I must have looked at him. I hate myself as Owen's dick pushes up against my prostrate, I hate the satisfaction I'm feeling now, I have the sweet sticky revenge I imagine against this creep, I hate me having that power, the power over his body, I hate it and I want it so much more, more even then this dick my ass in encircling, more than the freedom even to just escape these men, and I look behind me and he's got his eyes closed and I imagine the violence running through his head and is it so good as mine, is it? I can smell the metallic tang of the coppers Kevlar sausages, almost taste it on the tip of my tongue, and this process of divine rectal peristalsis suddenly lurches up a notch, faster, churning harder. Fuck me harder, Owen, ruin me, my body is saying, and I can feel shooting pains of pleasure running around me barrel-like, firing up to my chest, my throat, and down from my brain, pleasure of pain, of violence returning and they meet in the middle, in my gut, a dick in my asshole and killing around my eyes, and I exhale and exhale again and the sky is black now and is rumbling and there's no sun now and then. Then my thighs lose their strength, they start to shake and the rhythm of my bat matches the rhythm of this man's body and the point they meet, in the middle, in my stomach, my ass is fizzing up and I feel my ring get tight and fluid start streaming through my dick and he's shielding his face from this vicious attack and the room fills with a light, a crack of light from the window to the wall as my butt explodes with sensations and this policeman stops his struggle against me. A fizzing white noise fills my ears, dripping down my internal tubes like hot cocaine into my gullet, my throat is burning. The room is filled with energy: movement, noise, light: my eyes blur. London seems far away now; feet aren't connected to pavement, eyes aren't fixed down on phones, instead the heat of my ass is joined with that power that has hung over the city like a deluded smog all summer, an electric smog that keeps the rain away, that channels each sharp frustration towards the sky, and it's ending!

It's mine, my arse! Sleepless, wireless, pinned 100ft over the building sites, a mesh of bitter data, buffering social disorder, high up above the estates, amongst the England flags, my arse is transforming the atmosphere! I push back into the orgasm, my vision full white, and above me, an almighty roar of air, sucked out of my lungs, out of the room, the whole street, pulled up into the gathering clouds. Fag packets, fried chicken boxes, phonecards, pulled from the gutters, up into the storm: my body quivering with anal orgasm and the room is mine and the lightning that fills the room glows and my orgasm is gone and my violence is gone, retreating through the window with electricity and Owen is gone, collapsed on top of me and moving no more and I take a deep breath of the airless room. The city is rattled and changed, the sky bruise-purple with pure cop-hatred; my arse has done the impossible, punched murder into desire.

As I lay there, I felt sweat drip from my armpits, this rich humidity. The sheet was pulled up to my body on both sides

– I stared up at the ceiling, pulling the bedsheet from my sides, steadying myself, slowly bringing myself back from one world of power to this world of impotence. My skin was creamed; I felt his spunk tricking in rivulets up or down my asscrack, pooling around a hot little ring, mixing with our sweat, sending the bedsheet translucent like salty, fatty chip paper.

My mind was held to the ceiling, locked there by the thought of a fed with a cracked head, to the rich spunk stinking up my flesh good, god, to that fucking cunt with his bulging uniform crotch, that nauseous cunt, to the thundering train, to the thought of hot sticky blood caking in the black webbing, tainting his silver shoulder numbers, matting in the damp hair rolled in with the tumbling fat at the back of his neck. The heat was oppressive, the heat and the damp like we, me and him, were down deep, down a mine, with coaldust smeared across our white bits and our muscle strung tight. The noise, the noise was a lost ringing now. The thundering clattering freight train, the blood I could trace in veins of sound pumping across my eardrum, these sounds were gone. Just a plane of white plaster crossed by a crack, just an awareness of the man's presence on the mattress next to me, shifting weight as he re-dresses himself, just the stench and dribble of clumping semen sprayed around my body, just the pounding of fat little raindrops on the broad window panes.

CHAPTER 11

The shocking state of Britain's streets! A generation lost to a failed education system! The sick truth behind Britain's benefit timebomb! Street detritus! pavement dust, crisp packets, fag ends!

The strapline sits demurely in the bottom right corner of the hoarding, all lowercase, with typical English understatement, polite and self-effacing. "britain is shit - visit it!".

When you look around you, you realise your world is full of PERVERTS. Pete, I say, I know you struggle with your rent. I wish I could help. Never you say. Around you are high buildings and on the top of one blonde women who work very hard so why shouldn't they enjoy themselves enjoy themselves with some slightly older and some slightly younger men by drinking from what looks from the street like tall glasses but that could just be the perspective talking. They make you SICK because they are YUPPIE FUCKS blind to the crazy carnage austerity a campaign of mad TERROR is imposing on the streets below.

Pete I tell you people cannot necessarily be reduced to their jobs that's reductive and dangerous and perhaps even bigoted as I take a deep sip from my can of Red Stripe which you have always taken as something of a south London affectation but you disagree not even particularly respectfully because you are filled with the force of true conviction only an abiding belief in class slaughter can bring and you say FUCK OFF in a long drawl they are FILTHY YUPPIE SCUM and I hardly have to explain why. You take a sip yourself and realizing your beer is both warm and flat you pitch your remaining quarter-filled can toward the rooftop where it misses by quite a stretch but still manages to catch their attention.

OI! Comes the response not a market oi but a stock market oi less guttural more shackled to the back of your throat basically the oi you'd expect from THE SICK reality-denying SICKOS who frequent private members clubs what's your problem he might as well shout oik FUCK YOU your reply with admirable confidence straight from the diaphragm like YOU'RE ALL FRIGID CUNTS which I know you don't mean in a misogynistic way you never do but it comes across a bit like that but you should always write for your audience I think so it's probably a good call because it'll prove your credentials as a fearsome proletarian to these fucks I just hope you qualify it with some critical content something smart but instead you sort of bend your legs and arched back you hold your arms out and almost belch the word DESTROY! Perfect I think that kind of sums it all up doesn't it and at that moment I remember why I like you so much.

Unable to throw off the feeling of the copper on me, and of the breaking storm that followed that orgasm, I walked back to Bermondsey that night. The streetlights were back on, but as I walked I felt people's conversations were more tense. As I walked down Jamaica Road, groups stood around outside shops. People looked over their shoulders as they crossed the road. At the time, that incident in Soho felt like a one off but what happened later made me wonder if you hadn't planned it as part of the war, an opening salvo for well over a month of urban insurrection that only ended with the deployment of live ordinance. The death toll was admirably low considering the campaign of arson that followed, although risk management consultants later reported that fatalities could have been many times higher had the planned pedestrianisation of Old Compton St gone ahead in the mid-nineties. The original plan, which would have seen the street closed to traffic from Wardour St to Cambridge Circus included widespread use of paving in red and tan stock brick, much like Carnaby St and the risk consultants estimated that the utilisations of cobbles that occurred in the Rupert St/ Archer St area would have occurred right down Old Compton St. Anyone can throw a can.

CHAPTER 12

6 months sun. 6 fucking months. Her dad laughed her off when she said it was global warming. He didn't buy it, he said, as if it were for sale. But then cunts like Dad thought every opinion was for sale. He was a climate sceptic, or something. He had an acronym for it. GWM, or something. She had found his account on the newspaper message board, on the family PC, logged in to his account. Comment is Free.

She read his profile. He called himself "Right-thinking"... laughs... that made her laugh. "Right-thinking family man" or something. Not so many laughs. "Right-thinking family man, GWM" or whatever. What was the acronym? Global Warming Maniac. Masturbator. Mentalist, like. Great Wanking Maniac. Gross Wanking Madman. Maybe that wasn't the acronym. It should be, though. She stayed logged in to his account and left an obscene message under an article about Fern Britton. She hoped it would go some way to ruining his reputation amongst the CiF community. She read back the comment. It was fucking gross.

Scrolling through the CiF subpage these was an article about famous TV dogs, and one about sexual abuses and the elderly. She considered leaving another comment, eyes flicking from information to information. Too much data to focus on. She couldn't think of an idea. A joke. Not to worry, she pushed her orange juice between her teeth, I'll deface his profile, maybe. She looked at it again. "Right-thinking" what a dick. Hadn't even changed the default avatar, after 8 months of commenting on the site, increasingly, addictively.

It was the first thing he'd do when he got home from work, as part of his log-in routine, especially if her mum was still out. He did it at work, too, and she knew because she checked it when she was at school. She knew his username, and she followed him laboriously, obsessively. She'd run her cursor down each page during lunch and trace his stupid opinions on halal food or the England football manager or gay marriage or social workers or McDonalds stores or Nicholas Sarkozy or the U.S. Primaries or traffic calming measures or public sector pension reforms or Kim Kardashian or female genital mutilation or Billy Bragg or fuel prices or changing British tastes in breakfast or Top of the Pops or motorway services or job cuts in the postal service or job cuts in engineering in the North-East or job cuts in the immigration service or your opinion on the next round of strikes or women on the frontline or new trends in erotica or Tony Blair's career after he was Prime Minister or Nick Clegg: future leader? or war in Syria or the EDL or Trotskyists or education cuts or Martin Scorsese or TOWIE or gay pride or animal rights or the bus service or Bob Crow or U.S churches or spousal abuse or the proliferation of chicken shops in London or paedos or car insurance or rape. She knew all of his opinions on these subjects, and more. He was a man, a made man, a white man, the baseline of opinion, the rightful holder of opinion, the person for whom opinion was a solid state, a default, a man used to being heard, a man.

Over the last year, she guessed she'd learned more about him from his comments than from the previous 16 years, living under his roof. There was nothing outwardly violent about the man, nothing on his skin that marked him out, or in the tone of his voice or smell of his breath. If she had to list the reasons she'd used to come to hate him, she's not sure she could. There was an atmosphere to the man, though, a residual film that coated him, of cynicism, of fear masked with petty unpleasantness, of a *limit* he didn't want to surpass.

The more she read, the more she realized her initial hunch was right. He *was* a wanker. A car revved its motor outside, and she shifted herself towards the window, pulling her school skirt down where it had ridden up her thighs. She had felt sexy today. Kinda sexy in the mirror. Pleased to see the looks, this time. It wasn't her dad's car; it wasn't her dad's car she was waiting for. He'd gone up to Swindon for the weekend. As he'd left he'd kissed her goodbye, sort of on the forehead, but at the same time as he left her a list of instructions. Things to do before mum got back. He did the same whenever he left the house, and she resented it somewhat. Like the handing out of tasks was more spontaneous than the affection. She hadn't done the jobs yet, anyway.

It wasn't mum, though. Mum would be back

later and Chubz, her big brother, was taking advantage of Dad's absence to visit his mother and sister in the Medway urban conurbation. He was due in about now, in a taxi from the station. I was sorry to disappoint sis but I'd gotten a later train. I'd been held up. In work, maybe. Or at Elephant and Castle. Or maybe the train was late.

My sister liked me and I like her. We had proper conversations, despite the 8-year gap. Because of it. She looked through the PVC windows. Through the godawful fake diamond leading. They'd been like that when we moved in. Across the short green lawn, the cracking pavement, a taxi had pulled up. But it wasn't me.

She sat back at the family PC. Her comment was still there. 14 recommends. A bit gross, she thought, that I can even imagine that. In the past year or so my sister has got angry. I liked that - angry young women. Young women who aren't angry are stupid, I thought. Because *look* at this place. As she logged out she thought about her dad. And his *opinions*. He treated the world like his home, that same attitude.

His house, his rules. It was his rules that ran everything, as far as she could make out. Everywhere, dads, modulating, tempering, steering.

For both of us Dad/s was a gas that filled the air - a household gas who choked us. Dad/s was a gas that had seen it all before, a gas that thought "not to worry - it will blow over". My sister and I didn't talk much about him, but there was certainly a feeling that what was happening was different, that he hadn't taken into account the little things we see not because we're young but because we're always awake and never comfortable. We attuned, sis and me, whilst dad thinks we zoned out.

A wasp was slamming against the window pane with relentless force, rattling the frame. The taxi door slammed. A man with thick boots and a waxy, long, grey-brown coat dashed from the taxi to a house across from ours. He was sweating from the heat, one of the few men still dressed up so smart long since most banks had told their staff they could wear shirt sleeves, and had turned off the air-con, now bills were running too high. On the doorstep he rearranged his cuffs before ringing the bell.

I didn't come home. Instead I was leaning over the balcony of the flat. For weeks police had upped their patrols round the estate, claiming a rise in anti-social behavior, which meant we were sitting outside too much for comfort I guess. I'd gone through my wardrobe, thrown some things in my blue gym holdall; a nice blue jumper, some jeans, adidas hoodie, aussiebums, socks from american apparel. The lino of the flat felt so good in weather likes this, and I shifted barefoot and topless through the living room and out on the balcony, feeling warm air brushing past my nipples, listening to two stereos out on balconies. Their soundclash hit the block opposite and bounced down into the basketball court, down in the middle of the blocks. Lads had been playing there for weeks, younger kids buzzing about on bmxs, girls chatting and people walking up and away quickly, one guy follows, returns later, deal done. It would fill up later as people got back from work, more friends chatting, the Met would do a circle, zoots behind back, hassle for drinking, a peaked hat straight on the rare occasions they left their cars. Boxy silver vans would come later, crawling round the square, eyes peering out as people sat on their balconies and peered back. If they are so scared of this place, why do they keep coming back?

I sparked up a fag, flicking ash down the 5 floors below. From the block opposite Neil came out in his neat blue shirt and shorts, red bag swinging from the broad shoulders. Neil was the only guy I'd fucked on the estate, and still did sometimes; he was a postie, one of the cheerful ones, and seemed to know everyone on the estate; the first time I went round to his he told me he'd been bought up in one of the other blocks, but his parents, Nigerians, had died in the 90s. I'd guess he was mid 40s or some, and he was good with conversation, offering me a beer, letting me stick around and watch tv with him after I'd sucked him off on his sofa. He looked up at me and waved, and I waved back, and he hopped the fence and turned off down the street. I must have stood there for 20 minutes, feeling the sun prickle my eyelids, feeling the baking heat run across my knuckles as I watched people down below, and looked through the gap in the buildings at the early evening sun casting these long shadows across the borough. I pulled another fag out of the packet and cupped the lighter from the warm wind.

The fag smoke was too hot even at this time of the day; I ground it into the balcony railing and dropped the long butt into the flowerpot, muttered a bit, deep out breath. I could hear sirens in the distance, and closer ones, 3 or 4. As I turned to finish packing, into the cool dark interior of the flat, a string of silver riot vans emerged from behind the block on the north of the square, just for a second, before diving back behind the other block and down into Jamaica Road. Something was kicking off, I knew that when Neil bolted round the corner, behind him 10 or 15 more people, and from around the other corner the same number of feds, cutting him off from his flats. He ran through the square, across the grass, through where the dealers usually sat, jumped the wall and careered into the door of my building. He slammed the door code and disappeared inside; outside the feds had two kids on the ground, in restraints, a knee to the head and the back, visors down, zipties pulling their wrists together. 5 or 6 of them stood with batons drawn as the square emptied; a woman opposite shouted from her balcony. As they dragged the lads into the van, the blocks all looked at each other, balcony to balcony; a quiet conversation, tense and punctuated by more sirens across the borough, and dogs barking in lines.

A bang in the corridor, close. 3 more bangs, on my door. I opened it up and Neil was there, panting from the stairs and smiling too.
– Fucking hell Chubz, can I come in?

At the far end of the corridor the Sri Lankan couple were looking down the hall. Kasun smiled at me; he was in his early 40s but his smile always gave him a cheerful youth; he raised his hand and gave a brushing gesture. It was a strange validation for offering a lover a place to breathe, and I couldn't help but smile back, running my hand across Neil's back as he stumbled in. He collapsed on the sofa. I turned on sky news, stared for a minute at it, then stared at him. He was pumped, his hands ran back through his hair and he fucking winked at me, a fighter's wink. I dropped the remote onto the leather by his knees, and he let out his deep, friendly chuckle.

— Fucking hell Chubz, I don't know what just happened

— What did just happen?

I asked

— I... I dunno, but fuck I'm horny

One of his feet touched the floor, the other was hitched up on the end of the sofa. His legs were hairy, his calves broad, and my eyes led up his thighs like a V. He had a visible erection through his shorts, and they were damp, running down to his trousers

— You've pissed yourself Neil

He followed my eyes to his dick

— That's cum mate

— and where's your postie bag?

My eyes caught his; there was a flash of remembering, and he laughed as he exclaimed

— fuck! I left it there

He burst into a deep laughter and threw his head back; a gurgled mania as he grabbed his dick, a half-theatrical cackle through a breathless throat, the laugh of a teenage gang after a broken window.

– Skin up
   I said
– whilst I get you a drink
   I could still hear him catching his breathe
from the kitchen, spinning the teabag round
the cup. As I walked through he'd started to
build a joint, and looked up
– I dunno Chubz, it was crazy. I was up by the
end of St James' Road and these three police cars
had blocked the street. One of them had the
windscreen done in, and three of the policemen
had batons out, they were fucking hyped man.
   He was crumbling weed into the little valley of paper in front of him
– and this fucking fat one was red faced, and
5 or 6 youth were just dancing back and forth
in front of him, going like "come on, come on
then" and there were like 40 or 50 people all
crowding round and that
   I looked down as he started to roll the zoot
back and forth
– yeah thanks for this
– no, no worries babe
– then he just went for them, like bought his
nightstick right round, once, twice, pow pow,

135

they laughing at him yeah
— then what
— then he cracked one of the kids across the head, straight on, knocked him BANG to the floor, but by this time two vans had pulled up. Fuck knows what started it tho
— was he hurt
— yeah I dunno man, I think so - went straight down, but the fat fucker, he just goes for him on the floor, and cracks him across the legs, but this time

The half-rolled zoot caught between thumb and forefinger, he lets one had go and draws it up and across his body, about to strike someone
— this guy beats him down, pow across the back of his head
— fuuuuckkk

Neil licks his lips, then runs his tongue up then down the sticky edge of the skin. He's smiling still, his wide cheeks pulled up, and I start to feel my bellend against the edge of my pants. He's a beautiful man, his skin warm even from a distance somehow, and the tight short hair running from his neck up is starting to grey around the temple a bit. The pause for wetting the paper is over.

— right down, and the cunt is just flat out on the road

His eyes catch mine, to check I'm following, and his glinting smile is met by mine, half bashful, as I think about his dick down there, just waiting for me. He twists the paper in on itself and zips up the joint with a flourish.

— but then I feel weird, just... kinda a throbbing sensation, right up my arsehole

— what?

— Yeah I dunno what it was, just this like... I felt like I was getting fucked, but in the best way, know what I mean

— Fucked in the arse?

— Yeah like I was being fucked in the arse, like a hot throbbing up in my stomach

— What

— and this guy who smacked him round the head, he just looked up at everyone, and the other feds didn't react

— then he just put the boot in, kicked him hard as he could, and the moment he did it, I felt it again, in my stomach, but it felt even better this time

— What the fuck man

— Yeah fucking mad, but this is the weird thing yeah

— I looked at the young bucks yeah, who'd been kicking off, and they were like... grabbing themselves, one literally holding his arse like he'd just shit himself, and open mouthed and that, just smiling

— Then what?

— Then one of them booted the copper, bang, right in the head

There was a scrolling ticker running across the tv screen, and I caught the end "IN HACKNEY, REPORTS SUGGEST"

— yeah?

— Yeah, and his mates go in, even with other police *right there*, just crack him, and he's bleeding, but in the crowd, people are just clutching their stomach like, and this one guy has his dick out, right out his pants, like nothing mattered. And as the old guy, he just brings his foot down on the fed, I fucking came in my pants Chubz.

He's holding the joint between his lips and gesturing towards that dick running down his trouser leg, his wet postie shorts

— everyone was just fucking moaning, right there! Like no-one knew what the fuck was going on. Two of the feds were running for the guy on the floor, but he was fucking done in bruv, just blood and stuff, and the other feds, from the van, just stared at us, and we just looked at them, then it was like we all woke up. Adrenaline or some shit

— we bolted, they chased us, scattered, and more vans arriving, and then yeah, I ran, because they were after us, and came here. What the FUCK man.

He lay back against the pleather

— what the fuck.

He leaned forward and grabbed my lighter from the sofa arm. I'd never seen him like this; he was normally so relaxed, but now his blood was pumping hard. He sparked up, and took a deep drag on the zoot, turning his head to me

— and you know what

— I came so fucking hard. What the fuck.

— I don't really understand, Neil.

He passed to me, leaning back, and I grabbed his bare knee, running my thumb up across his hair

— was *everyone* coming?

— I don't know, but other people were, for sure. Those young guys were, for sure. Don't ask me to explain it Chubz, but that was what was happening.

He looked different now, less panicked than when he arrived, and broadly smiling

— what were they kicking off about

— I dunno bruv, but their car was *fucked. up.*

From the open balcony door we could hear a helicopter buzzing Southwark. The TV was flicking over now to shots from the air; we could see our streets picked out as news. There were groups of people gathering, and ambulances, and more and more cops arriving. No interviews, no-one on the ground, just clumps of bodies growing at intersections, just reports through twitter, just people and misinformation.

Neil stayed there for the rest of the evening; he made some food as I rolled another; I opened the beers I had left in the fridge. My flatmate Nadine was away for the weekend with her boyfriend near Epping, so we sat there in our own smoke, watching it getting whipped out of the window into the red sky. More helicopters arrived; 2 Met, a news one. When the news turned on to something else, we went to the window, to see more smoke or more blue lights. An occasional noise filled the square below as people ran back or forth. Neil asked to stay; as we lay back the news fed us more information.

An incident had kicked something off. A man appeared on the screen ducking behind a car. He must have been just metres away from us. Other cars in the background burnt. His northern burr tempered what he said, recounted stories of heat and anger, of an inevitability, of increased patrols. It cut to live footage; the reporter held his mic close to his chest whilst gesturing out behind him; he seemed sympathetic to the crowd, who were gathering near the Town Hall, and a pace to his voice as the camera swung up to catch the smoke drifting up into the sky.

— This is no carnival atmosphere. People here are angry; angry at police patrols, angry at the response of authorities, but most of all

His pause was interrupted by a bang, his head turned quickly to the side

— angry at poverty. With there being no end in sight to either the heat or the poverty, what happens next depends on the police response

another bang, and the camera swung with the reporters head. The riot squad had crashed through the crowd, and people dispersed past the reporters, as long plastic shields charged into the group. The return to the studio was delayed; the reporter jumped off his position to get through the crowd, swaddled around the quickly rebunched police; the noise was loud, deafening even, and crowded up to the in-camera mic. It had a focus - as the police retreated to their vans, packed shields clattering, one had been caught out, too far into the crowd. He turned to run, his shield pulled from his hand. It filled the tv screen - a blue overall through a crowd of skin, topless and short shorted, and a missile over his head. As he reached the line of shields, another missile, a full can, exploding at the feet of the police line. Another missile as the line parts, up against the shield wall. And another missile, followed by the camera, as he is about to make it through; a direct aim, caught live, as a dark grey lump collides with the back of the riot policeman's neck, and he falls into the line of cops, ricochets himself and hits the floor.

Me and Neil watched, less than a mile away. The evening sun filled the camera with a richness of colour, like the atmosphere was suddenly thin and airless, and light burst onto the lens. His head hits the floor once, twice, and as it comes to rest against the pavement, my arsecheeks pull tight against the leather sofa, my spine tears up through my body. I feel my balls contract as red blooms over the chalky tarmac on the city street. I turn to Neil, whose fingers tear against the sofa arm, and his eyes are damp and his lips parted as he watches the cameraman push through the crowd, as he watches the policemen in the line drag his lifeless body away from the gathered people. I grab Neil's thigh, crossing the border between cotton and skin, and grip harder as a rush is unleashed in my guts, and my ring constricts, effervescent anal activity, a fizzing orgasm; no metaphors, no sunlight and birds, no flowers, no nature, but my body rich and fleshy feeling these rush of uncontrolled hormones, my body and Neil's, sat in this flat, in this tower block, located in a grimy city full of cops, a hot city, feeling this ecstatic pumping anal orgasm on this ripped leather couch, I pull his leg harder towards me and he grips my forearm, and on the screen we see a man in front of the camera drop to his knees and hug his stomach too, and my dick fills with semen and I can a powerful surge of cum shooting once, twice, three times from the leg of Neil's shorts, onto the lino in a thick string, and his stomach pumping at the core, his belly, round at the ends, inflating and exhaling as deep inside his prostate is pumping out hot ejaculate across my living room and the riot squad drag their dead comrade out of the scene. Around them, men cling to street furniture, gripping themselves, the mic picking up chants no longer, but orgiaistic flows, men's guttural cries wobbling on the bottom note as a wave passes through the crowd, a wave of powerful butt-focused instant sex release. For a moment there is stillness; a break in hostilities, a burglar alarm filling the space. And then a hail of missiles - sticks, cans, rock; a mad male fury tearing at the streets and benches, flowerpots, bins; anything not locked down is torn up, the whole infrastructure of the city, whatever can be found and turned into a makeshift weapon, in a hunt for the return to that fevered rectal sensation, and blood splattered state apparatus, their blood, not ours.

The reporter calls his producer;
– The murder of a policeman induces a city-wide spate of cosmic, effervescent anal orgasms leading to a spree of civic-minded cop killings.

Me and Neil spent the night out in the streets. My sister watched back in Medway. Dad had an opinion.

CHAPTER 13

Over two weeks, the city battled in fabrics. The bold polymers of the hoardings remained, but blocks and strips of markings and colours delineated territories and space.

A strip of colour was tied high on a flagpole.

It hadn't been there last night. It wasn't an official job. I try to imagine the process of raising it. A ladder would have been needed, for sure. And the lamppost was aluminium, I think. It was raining last night, the pavement is still slippy, slippery. So another person must have been in on it; one to hold the ladder at the base.

The other climbs it. It's resting against the lamppost on a rung, not on one of its legs, so it rocks, sways, as the pressure of one leg shifts as it lifts a step or two. The girl is panting. Her arms are exposed to the rain. It isn't really summer rain, it's 6 months old, waiting to fall. She has the materials shoved up her vest; to Tom below it looks like she's pregnant, or a boy pretending to be pregnant, a pillow stuffed up his shirt. To her, it feels like she's pregnant too, but more keenly. She's sweating, he's using his body weight to steady the rocking ladder, bracing his shoulders against it, arms locked. The closer she gets to the top, the more pronounced the rocking. She looks left then right.

Horrible, a sinking feeing, like the ladder is slipping. What if someone (a police) comes? But the ladder isn't slipping. At the base, Tom has his head down, his empty mouth pressed up against his forearm. There's no rocking. She's struggling more but there's no rocking. She fights with a roll of gaffer tape, then a tearing sound, a forced zip, as an arm-length emerges. She rips it, then again, and has two arms lengths stuck to her forearm. Fumbling, she drops the roll, which bounces across the wet pavement, rebounding from the granite shopfront and rolling into the occasional traffic.

One piece of tape affixes to the top of their flag, and adheres straight to the lamppost. The second folds in on itself. She butterfingers presses what she can of the tape into contact with pole or fabric. She clatters down the ladder which detelescopes and, checking everything, they rush down the road. From the end of the street it looks ok, at night. Pixelated. What is a flag for, I wonder.

All this flag-waving tweaks me, freaks me out. I identify as red neon reflected in wet asphalt and I use the pronouns now/nearby/online. I suspect true allegiance lies in something a little more transient, as it should; in pink newsprint or the cheap bulk of glossy culture magazines.

These bastards were an ultra-femme bunch of anarcho-sissies, no real analysis, a loose collection of obscure injokes and anime pictures, no strategy to speak of. One of many gangs of faggots and new-found butt-pilgrims sprung up since the death of PC Ball, the poor putz slaughtered on the street, cut up like Serrano ham as cameras looked on, wild-eyed gangs, hot-boys, cool-customers armed to the teeths, arse-bandits in the truest sense, hunting for quick pleasure by turning street after street into an ambush. The flags are for bait, purple bait fringed in gold. The trap set, sits, getting damp in the pissing rain. These saboteurs crouch behind the private bins, locked against rats and skipdivers. Sweaty leather pulls against their thighs, they flick an obscene hand gesture up towards an open window towards a darkened room.

Drain gurgles rat the base of the flagpole. From the adjoining street you can hear a revving engine. The punk kids have unzipped, are masturbating each other in anticipation, preloading, fingering each other's cunts, chewing fat lumps of hash dipped in pro-biotic yoghurt, licking spindly tattooed fingers, frigging more, feeling a cold wind filling their boxers, and the wind fills the flag, its gold frill and purple ground, its puckered hole right in the centre, fist-sized, torn open and stitched around with lengths and lengths of gold thread, snaps of broken thread, fat lines covering each other, and the wind whistled through this ham-fisted gesture of an arsehole, pulling it through the pisswet night, the petrol sky, the wet shiny glass of office buildings reflecting flickers of the burning city torn apart by big hairy hetero men driven deadly wild with hot anal desire.

Once gay desire becomes universal the need for independent, separate so-called "straight culture" will disappear, become meaningless, wither and die. We all want the same thing, I think; hot wet anal pyrotechnics.

From the corner an echo rattles down the

street; crunching, sweating, shaking feds, equipment clatters like footsteps on gravel. The two lily-livered sissypunks, ultra-femmes, push their backs against the wall and hold their pants. The streetlights themselves were switched off days ago; flashlights appear at the end of the street - a troop of 8, stop a while, a murmled command and run batons brandished. Heads wrapped in fabric, coated in Kevlar, and rain lashing the bins and tapping on the helmets and the ccrrcht-crrcchhht-frenol-prsent-doy-ou-recive-over radio noise means not a rustle from the street can't be heard, they can't be heard, the faggots can't be heard the scraping of the barrel filled with concrete can't be heard pushed from the top floor window can't be heard nothing but police can be heard, police and equipment can be heard but not the concrete barrel twisting in the air, not till it lands it can't. Then it's heard like a cannon as it hits the last in the troop, exploding with a dust cloud which sticks to the pools of blood running across the pavement. The punks run from the building and from the bins, buckling at the guts with a furious pleasure as their arse goes off again, 3rd time today, such joy.

The next day there's a strip of fabric high up the lamppost, blue and white tape blocking my path down the road, all cleaned up but for the grey concrete dust sitting on the bin lids.

CHAPTER 14

The air and water system that kept the bunker temperate and habitable clunked and crashed in the spaces over Nigel's head, like beams inside the great Ship of State, being tossed about the wild tempest of rectal pleasure above. The rest of the cabinet, their secretaries, the civil servants, cooks and maids had probably been asleep for hours now. Only Nige stayed awake, unable to rest himself, and a few of his bodyguards, whose quiet pacing crossed past the doorway to his private quarters with clockwork regularity. He had dismissed the Metropolitan Police's official bodyguard; their loyalty was compromised, with dissent reaching deep in to the ranks. Best not take your chances with such cold-blooded killers, that was Nige's take on the subject. Here, 50 metres below an unnamed golf course somewhere in the Home Counties, the situation to our Nige looked unpromising.

Earlier this evening he'd taken a phonecall from the King, who, despite the pleadings of his courtiers, had remained in Buckingham Palace during the unrest. He had set up a telescope looking out from the window his chambers, according to his Undersecretary, and locked the doors. From his vantage point, with strict orders not to be disturbed, HRH watched the violence unfold. When a traffic policemen in ceremonial uniform had been mobbed on the Mall earlier in the week, his body left with white cotton gloves stuffed in his mouth and two of his silver buttons placed over his eyes, one on his tongue, His Majesty had seemed particularly upset, his noisy grief audible from the end of his Royal corridor.

The phonecall had not gone well. His Majesty had taken a close interest in events, and was frank and forthright in his anger, a position he had made extremely clear. The situation was untenable, he had said; he expected order and control to be back in place in London within the week, or... the serious threat wasn't made explicit to Nige, but he was aware things were as bad as they got. Perhaps a military council would rest control from Parliament, Nige thought. Perhaps I've blown it, blown it for good. The democratic experiment might be over for good, he thought. He slumped in to the ergonomic office chair and swirled the Dubonnet around the glass. This was his sixth glass tonight. He'd undergone a horrific shoot with a photographer from the *Sun* earlier in the evening, one requiring him to eat a plate of sausage and mash, washed down with a pint Victory Ale, as he plotted out fictional police actions on a giant A-Z of the capital. The indigestion was killing him; he'd already supplemented his digestif with 3 rennies, but the Lincolnshire pork was playing merry havoc with his guts, and the bunker was unforgiving with the result. He downed the drink, leaving the glass to roll from the desk to the floor. His three loyal little Daschund, Martin, José and Herman, ran to lick up the residue as it stuck into the carpet. Dissolute, Nige could barely bring himself to shoo them away.

He thought back over the preceding months; the joyous, shocking landslide of early May; his arrival into Downing St, his motorcade led by a purple and gold battlebus, Land of Hope and Glory blasting from loudspeakers atop its roof. The creeping withdrawal of the PC Brigade! The end of repressive European working-time directives! All this, and months of blazing sun, beaches full of Brits, haymaking indeed. This had meant to be a UKIP summer, he was sure of it. Yet, with only a page of manifesto pledges full-filled, the Kipper Revolution not yet in full swing, and mayhem ruled the country's streets.

Parliament had been recalled earlier in the week. At a special debate on the uprising, the Leader of the Opposition had had Nige pinned against the wall. A whirlwind of blonde, the electric Etonian had the Dulwich dullard thrashed to within an inch of his life. A vote of No Confidence followed, his backbenchers deserting his sinking ship. How had all the former Mayor's riot contingencies been allowed to lapse? Why weren't the water cannons enough? When was he going to do the right thing and bring out the army? Nigel collapsed under the barrage; under-briefed, his humiliation broadcast to the nation. A confidence vote had been scheduled for the following morning.

Nevertheless, Nige was stoic, if not upbeat. Retreating to his office for a quick sniff of the good stuff, he felt confident that a rousing speech, a Churchillian call-to-unity, and he could be back in charge. Once more into the breach! he joked to Melissa as he left the chamber for his waiting motorcade. Upon arrival at Downing St, however, he spelt a familiar scent, at once dread and arousing. Where had he smelt that before, he thought. As he pushed the office door open, the flash of blonde hair and black leather hit him like a sucker punch. Sat astride his desk, knife delicately flicking away detritus from between her perfect teeth, sat Gutrot Essenem. He let the door slam behind him.

— Gutrot!
  He exclaimed
— It's... it's such a pleasant surprise to see you here!
— Cut that crap
  Gutrot replied
— You have some explaining to do
  Nige pulled his tie, a ligature now around his bulging neck
— And explain I can
  He gulped
— What... what would you like to know?

— It's been 5 months since you were elected as Prime Minister

Gutrot barked

— And yet still, we are no further towards our new drugs landscape. What is your explanation, Mr Farage?

This was the first time she had addressed him so formally since the night they had met.

— Ahh, well, it's politics, you see. I had to make some decisions

With a snap her butterfly blade clasped shut in her hand. Nige gulped

— Gutrot, you must understand, I couldn't push through all my legislation at once. I had activists to please! The party faithful!

— And your relationship to them is worth more to you than there, is it? I see

She flicked her hair behind her ear and sat up from his desk

— No no no

Nigel gushed

— It's simply a matter of making sure we can get it through! We have to make sure the first bill withdrawing EU legislation gets through! But can't you see, if the Bendy Banana and

157

Human Rights Exemption (Foreigners) Act doesn't pass, what chance has the Poppers Freedom Act got? Can't you see, Gutrot? It's a matter of practicality!

— Nonsense!

Barked Essenem

— Nonsense of stilts! Nonsense nonsense nonsense! We chose you, Nigel, because you were a man of action! You promised a do-ocracy! And end to the Westminster elite!

— I am a man of action!

— No Nigel you are another metropolitan fancy man!

— I am not!

Nigel shot back, an air of anger inflecting his voice with a sudden, surging confidence, something he immediately regretted

— I am sorry, Gutrot, but I must assure you, our pact remains as strong as ever! Nothing could be higher on my priorities than returning an Englishman's right to isobutyl nitrite (2-methylpropyl nitrite). This is not a game for me!

Essenem was pulling her coat back over her shoulders, and fixing herself to leave. Nigel followed the silver chain around her slender

Flemish neck, plunging deep between her breasts. He looked at the little Balenciaga over-night back at her feet, and knew it was packed full of those joyous little brown bottles. He gulped down again. Gutrot followed his line of sight down to her bag, and back up to his eyes. They caught each other's glance

– You have forfeited our confidence, Nigel. I have discussed this with my team. I'm afraid we can no longer support you.

A sudden rush of panic ran through his body.

– And now this latest... situation... has emerged, we have decided our interest lay elsewhere. They lie with the real English people. It is obvious they would be receptive to the benefits of isobutyl nitrite (2-methylpropyl nitrite). It has become clear where the real power lies in this country, Mr Farage. It is not in Westminster, either with the old guard or your grocers and golfers. It is in the streets! Change must come from below! We were right the first time!

Her voice shook him. He felt his body seize up. In his head he ran a mental inventory of his remaining stock. 30, 50 bottles max. Bare-ly a day and a half of his fighting juice left;

the liquid had propelled him from a national punchline to a seat at the table with President of the United States. He needed it; more of it each day, from 2 or 3 bottles when he stunned the continent, to now... now, with it out of control. His hands were shaking at the thought of his rapidly depleting stock.

— Please. Please Madame Essenem! I can assure you, there is no higher cause for me than our liberty! But you must trust me! Power does not lie in the streets! If this anarchy is left unchecked - if you support it, Gutrot - a steady supply will never be guaranteed! Chaos, Madame, sheer chaos! We will turn into the Somalia of room odorisers! I must insist that you give me one more chance! I have plans being enacted as we speak!

The last lie slipped off his tongue without his even intending it to. Gutrot Essenem looked at Nige, then back down to her bag. Outside No. 10, sirens cut apart the afternoon air. A stench of burning police vans was clawing its way through the filter air-con of his private offices. Their eyes fixed upon each other's, and Nige did his best shot at steely.

— Very well, Nigel. I feel perhaps we have a bond, and you should give a friend his one last chance

Nige's shoulders dropped in relief.

— But I think you need a little incentive

she said, leaning down and gripping her bag by its thick leather handles

— I had bought you this as a parting gift

Unzipping the bag, a cornucopia of brands filled Nige's wide eyes. It was all there, all the good stuff - Rush, Liquid Gold, Ram, Locker-room. She'd even bought the really hard European gear; glinting as they rubbed up against each other, bottles of Fist and FF,, export strength stuff. He felt a buzz just looking at them, but also a warmth, touched that Gutrot, despite her steely Brussels exterior, would deliver such a gift as her parting present. He reached out to grab the bag, but she swung it from his reach, zipping it shut.

— Ah!

She snapped

— This, Nige, is reserved. On hold. I will return when you have fulfilled your side of the bargain. Until then, we shall not meet again.

Pulling the Balenciaga under her arm, she made for the door. Nige reached out for her, but she had already reached the stars. He realised his vision was blurring. His headache had returning, that sharp, spiky drill into his forehead. He ran after her, watching as his butler opened the big black door. She turned, and caught his eye, and he knew it was futile as she shot a glance that gripped him as hard as any divine poppers high. And she was gone. Nige crumbled on the landing, head spinning uncontrollably.

The rest of the day had been a rush for Nigel. He took a hit - a whole bottle of Blue Boy - from his remaining stash, wrapped up in a Fortnum and Mason's tote in his bottom drawer. That gave him the strength to summon his advisors and the heads of the military and elected Police commissioners from across the country. For hours they bashed their heads together, assessing and reassessing the situation, making contingency plans, but nothing convincing came together. The fury of the British butt-lust was too much, the boys in blue were tired, their morale dropping. It had become clear that

Doncaster, Scunthorpe, Canterbury were falling out of police control. Nige was getting increasingly agitated as he felt the rich nectar degrading in his bloodstream. My god, there must be an answer! He thought. But he had played his cards. The inability to wrest back Hull from the arse-bandits, even after deploying live ammunition, was a terrible sign. A great sense of foreboding overcame Nutty Nige. He raged on, reducing the Chief Constable of Thames Valley to tears with an ill-tempered assault on his manhood. He struck out across the War Cabinet, covering Douglas Carswell in a shower of Tizer. At last, he dismissed the team at 10pm, chasing them from No. 10. He returned to his private quarters, grabbed his red case, and ordered his security team to ready his chopper.

— Scramble the RAF escort,
  He barked
— we're going to Frimley Green. NOW!

  5 hours later, and here he still was, mulling over his rise to power, his heading days in the UKIP spring. He thought back further; those glorious years at Drexel Burnham Lambert where he felt the whole world was his oyster,

or Credit Lyonnais Rouse, where the wine never seemed to stop flowing.

— Once,

he thought

— once, I was the future of Europe. And how
what? I sit here like a defunct currency, heavy
in the pockets of the electorate. A liability. As
useless as a non-binding bilateral treaty.

He looked up to his framed picture of the
Baroness, whose stern eyes shot a sense of be-
trayal back at him. Damnit! How did this happen? How did I tank so disastrously at the first
opportunity? How did Farage - Farage, of all
people! - fail so dismally when presented with
his first real accountable position of responsi-
bility?

He knew his promise to Gutrot was empty. He was spent; anyone could see that, and
he wondered why Gutrot believed him. Perhaps there was more than pure practical politics
going on, he thought. Perhaps that first night,
she had felt what he had felt, somewhere deep
down. He was a little taken aback. Perhaps...
perhaps she *trusted* him.

The thought cut too deeply. It was there,

beneath the Baroness, for the first time in 30 years, that Nige stooped his head and began to weep. At first, just little tears, for himself. But as the enormity of the situation began to grasp, great crashing teardrops fell from his cheeks, dampening the front page of that day's Daily Telegraph, its headline emblazoned: "Farage Fiddles Whilst England Burns". Herman leant sympathetically against his paisley pyjamas.

Having composed himself, and fortified with a stiff drink of Ratzeputz, he decided he needed a firm and decisive act as leader. He wasn't going to be remembered as the Baroness, brought down by her own side. He lifted his heavy red case on to his desk. For a moment he left it unopened, instead tracing his finger around the seal of state, the great slamming portcullis behind which his dream of a New Britain lay trapped. Then he span the numbercode locks till the teeth released and the clasps sprang open. Lifting the lid, his remaining brown bottles sat before him, neatly sorted in order of nation of origin and held into the lid of his briefcase with little elastic straps.

One by one Nige removed each bottle.

Arranging them before him, he carefully unscrewed each plastic cap, passing it once, then twice, under his nose, taking in the rich, happy chemical pong. He then placed it on his desk, before continuing the ritual, with each inhale the memory of his happy highs running through his head. Finally, his whole remaining collection sat in front of him. He pulled his case off the desk, neatly resting it to the right of his desk. The room was beginning to odourise gently; he knew he would have to work quickly, lest the scents entered the air-conditioning system and his security team became alerted to his plan.

His top drawer opened with a thud, making him jump, then pause as he watched his locked door. Was that his imagination, or did the handle just turn? You're becoming paranoid, he thought. He leant over to his iPod, and span through his music collection, looking for something suitable. Beethoven's Symphony Number 9 began to waft from his stereo, mingling with the heady scents. Suddenly, he felt relaxed, calm for the first time all day. Perhaps it's just the poppers, he thought. But he felt know that the pressures of Prime Ministership began to leak away. He reached in to his locked draw, past his old service revolver, and grabbed an engraved crystal beer tankard, gifted to him by the ladies of UKIP upon his election to the European Parliament in 1999. Holding it to the light, he looked over the engraving: a cut-glass Spitfire floating gracefully over Dover's White Cliffs. Above it, the words "Best Wishes Nigel"; below, the motto "Give the Huns Hell!" He laughed to himself, and remembered those simpler days before he left for the EU, when he thought cheddar was a delicious cheese.

Nige laid the tankard in front of him. One by one, he lifted each little bottle, and drained its contents into the glass. Each movement held made the next a little easier, till, before he knew it, the glass was full. He gripped the cold handle and lifted the pint of poppers; held it up to the Baroness, then threw his head back and gulped it down. It was, he mused, the first pint he had enjoy for almost two decades, and he chuckled to himself as he fell into that deepest and horniest of sleeps.

CHAPTER 15

The disorder was a physical manifestation of joy. There was some materialization of a relationship that he usually felt as a pressure behind his eyes. To see his residual migraine as a political force that was tearing, literally tearing up the fabric of society around him - street furniture, petrol station advertising hoardings, security shuttering, police vans - was fast-acting relief to the very site of pain. On the six streets around - from the estate, down to the off-licence and the school gates, to the junction - the only hi-vis was a thin strip on the periphery. The borough had never smelt, looking, felt quite so much like my social life. I couldn't quite... I couldn't. I was horny, but past fuckable.

Chubz walks through, between, streets. His feet kick through the detritus of our shopping spree - broken bottles, torn point-of-sale displays, and shoe boxes: islands of shoe boxes, piled to waist height. Blue, with white stripes.

The agitational fug is punctuated by a well-timed missile and everyone seems relieved not least the sweaty line of coppers in fire-retardants and rather than retreat the line of people most of whom are jobless pusch towards the tax-offices with a half-cheer.

Not a chance said Pete when asked if the worst of the trouble was over this is a technological city in revolt he liked the sound of that and the fact the Russia Today cameraman angled the shot at the point in order to catch the burning biffa bin behind him made his especially pleased and that night the metrics and analytics would seem to prove both right in their aesthetic collaboration. It seemed a shame no-one used the word "viral" any more.

The return of political violence and street politics has really livened up the European Experience in the last three years. Our metrics prove it compulsive with high loyalty and recognition factors. Street violence holds strong connotations with cosmopolitan Europe, youth subcultures and urban micro-communities. Causing physical damage to public property and serious injury to law enforcement officials is the closest we have to a counter-culture today. It is from within this cultural landscape that the influential and socially-credible aesthetic and consumer trends of the next 10-20 seasons will emerge. We strongly favour a policy of trend-focus and network analysis from within this territory.

When people talk about events like this, after the fact, they always draw on how expected it was. How there was a build-up, a pressure-cooker, a powder-keg. That wasn't how I experienced it. This was an extension of an everyday war that niggled like a verruca, that picked away at human flesh. It seemed all very routine.

CHAPTER 16

Horses have a way of keeping time at a standstill. When holding the line. Their hooves rise and fall with a sort of panicked grace. You become transfixed by them as they stand in line, treading water; they emanate a smell and a heat which is out of beat with the situation unfolding. I hesitate to say they are noble, but they are certainly at once removed from the public order situation that surrounds them: the arbitrary cordons and kettles whose purpose is disguised to all but the Commanders in the central control room.

The Commanders have metals attached to their names in these situations, which have become London's punctuation. Bronze, Silver and Gold, according to rank or role rather than success or failure. Cressida Dick was a Gold Commander when she ordered the execution of Jean Charles de Menezes, an electrician travelling to work. Bob Broadhurst was a Gold Commander when he oversaw the beating to death of Ian Tomlinson, a newspaper vendor returning from work, by a terminally aggressive member of The Force.

The way some people talk you'd think a tougher metal controlled all this. Linked this killing and that, linked this scene of violence to that. A public order kingpin. I've had enough managers to doubt the existence of the man who oversees the miscarriages of justice. It seems to me more likely that everyone is watching the balls in the air, and no-one is watching the clowns. If you took your eye off the balls, the passing of the buck from hand to hand, they'd all fall down, perhaps.

A pain rings across my shoulder. I look up to see that a mounted officer has pushed away from the line, into the crowd. His rubber-coated steel truncheon is rising for another swipe at me. I push into the crowd but the wall of bodies won't give, and the crowd judders, tripping over its own feet. I look to catch the officers eye, to show him I'm trying, really I'm trying, but there's a force behind me and it just won't let up. I feel stupid, fucking stupid, like a kid pleading with a teacher, and simultaneously like I've done something wrong and I'm just waiting for my dad to come home. A fluttering stupidity, like I'm reckless, and stupid, and shit, and sorry,

I'm so sorry, this wasn't a situation I ever intended to be in and I've really already learnt my lesson so please stop compounding my shame by repeating my crime and I'm breathless and shamed and slam I feel the baton again but not the pain just the shock because somehow *thank god* it has missed me and that black girl just there her hair matting with blood and it's *so* red and her voice is so red too.

I push one deep into the crowd. I wouldn't like to be that officer, I think, cos this girl's friends are fucking mad and screaming a blue streak across the top of the front line and *fuck me* they're going for the officer on the horse grabbing at the bridle this is fucking *awesome* and the crowd are going wild for it and there are two chants washing up against this, one of many epicentres "shame on you" from the left and "your jobs next" from behind and the right and I look up to the police officers face.

There is a visor coming from the blue helmet, ribbed with hi-vis. There is a mouthpiece under that and a balaclava under that and under that I can make out the eyes and the eyebrows are *plucked*. And I can't make it out –

despite their definition - with just eyes and plucked brows and what her expression is. I can't tell if that is terror or that is shame, but either way those are big things to deal with when you're sat on a horse. No-one ever got closure on a horse. And I can't tell what she's trying to do, what she's trying to control. Is she trying to regain control of the horse, which is increasingly terrified of the hands and the fireworks passing feet overhead? Or control of her own emotions which I hope are shame and fear but I hear are usually disgust and anger?

I think about her, and stop thinking about her. I pity her a bit. She's there and feeling this too: the exhilaration, the fear, and her own feelings I can't imagine; whatever feelings are stimulated by receiving payments to beat people who disgust you. All this, and on the back of a horse. The fierce girls sink back into the crowd who call for a medic.

I'm up against this wall of horse legs again, the tension down on both sides. Occasionally something is thrown from the back of the crowd and it clatters across the tough plastic shields of the people on the horses. The horse legs rise and fall and in the wall it's hard to distinguish which legs are part of which animal, so closely packed are they. Their hooves crack against the tarmac in an off beat rhythm, and they *steam*. Not just from the mouth and snout and arsehole but all over, in the cold and rain. All the equipment, hanging from them and their riders, clatters against their broad expanse, great pack animals of violence.

The texture of the crowd changed and her horse swang round against the body of the mob. I go to push back into the bodies, away from her and her sticks, but they give way I fall. Crowds dissipate behind you like that, without warning. And through the legs, I saw more legs, in boots and horses hooves, and dogs straining necks at leashes. The crowd was firing off, the kettle broken by some fierce clatter of biffa bins and sticks and thick scaffold. The tension in the air tore, and lungful of fresh cold winter evening filled the crowd with nerve and they *bolted* fast as fuck as half the cops pushed and the others fled.

I lift myself off the ground as the horses start to spin and reel on the spot, backing and pulled round by the military bridles, clattering eye visors on saddles and moving out, slapping, fast and scary.

Here was the function of that night; the six months 9 months, YEAR of ever increasing scuffles on the street, fights with cops and smashed up municipal and private property - the strange electricity generalized. I was pulled into a stream of crowd running like a fleet right then left through the estate and down the muddy green bank, the grassland that separated the estate from the road that dipped down past costcutters, all raging as sirens approached. We left them then, from behind the shop we heard shattering glass and eastwards the smell of rubber on fire, and we tucked eastwards, through the churchyard and out to the world.

That's how the night started, for me, pumped and horny as fuck. All bodies everywhere, all fleshy and clothed and pumped full of blood when the missile leaves your hand. People who are alive where 'alive' means open, even forced open, to possibilities beyond your control. Rich and loaded working-class bodies are pregnant. We are flesh and fleshy life and we are opposed to your written codes. I want to touch everyone around me - the girl breaking this window, the two boys who have pulled the fed from his car and are dismembering his useless body on the garage forecourt with fat erections struggling through their pants, with bodily fluid shuddering through them as their prostates swell with cop killing joy; pure joy. Our bodies, alive and pregnant in this group who charge around the street, are what separate us from the zombie dead that exist in the graveyard of screens. This is my strategy, I think, my strategy is bodily love.

The breakdown of security for the rich and powerful in London was tied so closely to our feet and legs and chests and arseholes I could only marvel. All change that happened was an inversion of the law of the feds; as it restricted our movement, and here now we ran unrestricted, not stopped and held and search and arrested in our tracks, but where we put our bodies mattered, for that night, for those months, for that time we were out of the shop and office. And finally that sweating fear of those around me, that gay fear of exposure and bodies uncontrolled began the lift off me; we were bodies here together and how we used them together like a diagram, a diagram of a process all linked, how my body worked with the body of the boy I'm next to - that became our politics because that's where power was.

As we tore from the graveyard loud thuds were followed by ripping as rubber ricocheted across the pavement and the tarmacked road and impacted in the bodies with us with a crunch of bone and warm damp patches. From smoke at the corner two, four, six full-length riot shields in haze like the shinpads in a wall shuffling to defend a free-kick, and from between them the thick stubby end of a projectile cannon. The crowd twisted and split as quickly as it came. Great black rubber hulks, corpses of cops strewn with sticky human goo, hung from streetposts already adorned with torn fabric, strung up by their belts and harnesses now stripped of weaponry. Between two fronts an alley carried us round behind the station and into the glow of new streetlamps. Edges of faces betrayed our sweaty features and these fat smiles, and the stench of burning rubber choked beneath the scarves that hid our features from the cameras, everywhere. The stench blew up the street. Blood pumping to my ear gave way to the crackling of paintwork on nearby shops. From the end of our street a car windscreen had been caved and flames poured from the front of the vehicle. Jewels of glass like CGI droplets covered the street, and that body was unmistakably Owen. Blue check shaded red-brown. He was gutted; I looked at his lifeless visage, and I thought back to all our nights together, and I looked for the regret, but I couldn't find it. The night's joy was too much. I admit it; I was chuffed.

I'm sorry Owen, but no malice, just militia.

POSTSCRIPT

You can't forget the panic of consummation, the burning streets, the 1000 ski masks with fat penises where the eyes of the loser militia should be.

The key to a happy, healthy life and sense of wellbeing is ensuring an intelligent relationship with your key life-brands. Keep your personal portfolio of brands fresh and balanced.

The feeling of being part of a mob bears little relation to its representation. At least, that's my experience. If you want to feel like an individual who has importance, join a mob. I enjoy situations of civil disorder because I enjoy watching people trying to kill each other.

The looter and the online pirate are the subjectivities with the clearest, most intuitive comprehension of the nature of contemporary semio-capitalism; they are the brand ambassadors, and if they cannot be harnessed they will overrun and destroy it. A strategy must be had for disempowering and utilising us: and it cannot be legislative.

These days I mainly cruise online, in the dark data terraces that slip between open tabs. When I suck a man off I always swallow. I enjoy the sensation of his DNA slipping down my throat; it is the most sensual form of data entry my life currently permits.

The strains and insults incurred through the day, the working day, that are pushed between the two of us. We can rework the social tensions of him, the white-collar yuppy, the buy-to-let landlord, the ethicist in the supermarket aisle, the profiteer and the privateer, the bastard, the nice guy, Mr Nice Guy, the nice guy who means well, and me, the 6-month let, 6-month contract, managed and manager - we can rework those tensions between thumb and forefinger when we peel off clothes, like blu-tak.

The working life of the new European millenial is not regimented according to time-and-motion studies; it is teased by the psychological rudder of management. It is nudged, silently, friendly-like.

The future extends to the end of my contract.

Chubz: The Demonization of My Working Arse
by Spitzenprodukte

© 2014 Spitzenprodukte and Montez Press
ISBN: 978–3–945247–10–5

Publisher:
    Montez Press
    Adenauerallee 46
    20097 Hamburg
    www.montezpress.com

Design: Max Prediger
Print: Druckhaus Köthen